The Lily Pickle Eleven

"You're sick," Mad Mave shouts. "Sick, Harris. Whoever heard of anyone wearing mushrooms on their heads?" and she stomps about, purple as a bursting plum with rage.

Mr Kendal looks at E. H.'s green and red head and he frowns a bit and then he says "But what do you wear them for, lad? I mean, why mushrooms?"

"Them's my, like, meaningful statement of life," E. H. tells Mr K. "If yer see what I mean?"

Mr Kendal said as he didn't rightly see what he meant, no.

"Well," E. H. starts. "Mould, that's what mushrooms is, innit?" and Mr K nods. "Well, then," Elvis goes on. "It stands to reason, don't it? Mushrooms is my, like, personal statement about life, like, mushrooms is mould, the world is, like, mouldy, yeah?"

This is exactly what E. H. is like. Brilliant.

The Lily Pickle Eleven

Gwen Grant

Young Lions

First published in Great Britain by William Heinemann Ltd in 1987
First published in Young Lions in 1990

Young Lions is an imprint of the Children's Division,
part of the Collins Publishing Group,
8 Grafton Street, London W1X 3LA

Copyright © Gwen Grant 1987

Printed and bound in Great Britain by
William Collins Sons & Co. Ltd, Glasgow

for Rebecca

Chapter One

I didn't think I'd ever want to write another book but here I am again, writing away like billy-ho and why? Because Mr Kendal has had another brilliant idea, that's why.

'Get that book out, Lily,' he says to me one morning. 'There's going to be new things happening around here. What! Stick with me and the sky's the limit. Kick-off!' he goes on. 'Football team! That's what I wanted to see you about,' and he fixes us all with a face that's like bonfire night – bright and shining.

'Oh, no,' I groan because the last time Mr Kendal looked like that, he started a Band and we had to be in it.

'We're going to have a bit of culture,' Mr K. says sharply. 'Culture. Got that?' he goes and everybody nods their heads.

'I like a bit of culture, myself,' Deirdre Summers says. 'Here, it ain't an animal, is it?' she asks Mr K. and he says, 'Certainly not.

What it is, Deirdre, is eleven brave and true lads.' He stares at us thoughtfully. 'And lasses, of course. Yes, eleven brave and true lads and lasses who make up a team: united, loyal . . .'

'Stupid,' E.H. puts in and Mr Kendal stops talking and fixes him with a freezing stare.

'Stupid! Stupid!' he goes. 'It's not them that's stupid, my lad. No, them as play together stays fit together. That's what we're gonna do. Us lot.' He waves an arm to show us. 'We're going to keep fit.' And he bounces up and down. 'Hup, two, three, four.'

'Yuk,' says E.H. and in two seconds flat, poor old Mr K. is left talking to himself.

'Where they gone?' he shouts. 'Come back here, you lot. Come back here.' And although I've got a fresh book out, I shouldn't think there'll be much to write in it. Not about a football team, anyway.

'Oh yes, there will,' Mr K. says firmly, tapping the side of his nose with his finger. 'Haven't you heard that old Chinese proverb?'

'Chicken fried rice?' Mavis Jarvis asks.

'First catch your football team . . .' Mr K. says, and half of M.J. slowly disappears round a corner. The other half Mr Kendal has hold of. 'Now then, Mavis,' he says. 'About this here team . . .'

Well, they call me Lilian Pickle, Lily for short and since I wrote my last book, I've got myself a Dad.

My Dad, Mr Pickle, left home when I was six and was never seen again, only across a crowded street, my Mam says, which was exactly how she wanted to keep it. And then we had the Band in the flats and here came Mr Pickle to see us.

'I shall return,' he tells my Mam and she straightway goes out and buys four new bolts and three window locks.

'Not if I have anything to do with it!' she tells Mr P. but he didn't listen. One morning he was not there when I went to school and then he was there when I got home in the afternoon.

'Hello, Miss,' he says when I walked in, so just for now I am living with my Gran, who keeps telling me about how her Grandad went over Niagara Falls in a barrel.

I do wonder if there's any chance of getting a job like that for Mr Pickle.

'You have to give him time,' my Gran tells me. 'He's turned over a new leaf and you'll just have to get used to it, my girl.'

I liked the old leaf best when Mr Pickle was underneath it.

Well, where I live with my Gran is in Rat Trap Flats, the only flats in the world made entirely out of spent matches and spit.

When you want to see what the weather's like, you don't bother looking out of the window, you just peer through the cracks.

'One flame and they'd go up like a bomb,' Mr Kendal says and you can see queues of folk night and day standing with a lit match against the walls.

'Burn, drat you. Burn!' they're going.

Rat Trap Flats are three blocks of flats that look exactly like a tip.

In fact, anybody who comes round here, they go, 'My word, I didn't know the tip was so near,' and fling their old double bed and washing machine straight through their car windows and drive away.

The bobbies are here that often, they're talking of pulling the flats down and building a police station instead.

'I wouldn't mind that,' my Gran says. 'If they'd only put a little post office in it, as well.'

I suppose they could put a little post office and a big bobby together. When all the Grans and Grandads fetch their pensions on a Thursday morning, they practically hire a machine gun to go with them.

They go down the pavement in a posse, rattling their walking sticks on the pavement and watching out for muggers round all the trees. (Two). (Trees).

This town, Workton, is on the very tip of Nottinghamshire.

'Mek sure tha dun't fall off,' them in Yorkshire say. 'And if tha does, don't fall this way.'

'We fire when we see the whites of yer eyes,' them in Derbyshire say.

We say we wouldn't be seen dead anywhere but here and they all point you in the direction of the nearest cemetery.

'Never put off till tomorrow what you can do today!' they tell you.

'There *has* been people who've got famous from here,' E. Harris says. 'And there's gonna be more because there's gonna be me for a kick-off.'

'Isn't that exactly what I was talking about?' asks Mr Kendal, coming smartly round the corner. 'Hup, two, three, four. You have kick-off when you has a football team,' and he beams at us all. 'A football team is the thing. That's what we need. By Jove, I'll say it is.' And jog, jog, he bounds straight back out of sight.

'You could use Harris as a goal post,' Mad Mave sniggers. 'He's skinny enough. Not like my Hoggy.'

That's certainly true. You'd need two goal mouths and there still wouldn't be enough room for Hoggy Morgan, with his spots and his size sixteen feet.

On the other hand, he'd fit into Mad Mave's mouth perfectly. Plenty of room there – and some to spare, as well. Every time she opens her mouth, darkness falls.

'Saturday afternoon,' roars Mr Kendal, appearing again like Hamlet's Dad. 'Be there. On the field. Two-o-clock.' And then he's gone again and Mave the Mouth and Hoggy have gone with him.

'You know what you were saying about being famous?' I say to E.H. when I think it's safe and he nods.

'Fame and I are old friends,' he drawls.

'Well, what do you think to me changing my name?'

'It depends what you want to change it to,' E.H. says. 'If you wanted to change it to Coal-Sack Carol, well, I'd have to think about it. On the other hand, if you wanted to change it to Tilly Tripe . . .'

'I wanted to change it to Daphne Floris,' I tell him and when he's crawled back onto his feet from off the ground where he fell laughing, E.H. says, 'Ho, very nice, I'm sure,' snigger. 'Daft Flo, for short, I suppose?' he says and then collapses laughing down a drain pipe.

'I'd rather be called Daphne than Elvis,' I

snarl but he slides rapidly out of the drain and says being called Elvis is like being a member of a Royal Family.

'Not our Royal Family, dope,' he goes, when I look sideways at him. 'If I was called Charles or Edward or Andrew, I'd need to be wrapped head to foot in fitted carpet and five pound notes. Nah,' he goes on. 'I mean a *proper* Royal Family. The Royal Family of the world. Them as can do things. People look at you when you tell them you're called Elvis, I can tell you.' And he smiles like a little shark.

'I don't think that's why they're looking at you,' I say, because, personally, I think anybody with a completely bald head painted green and edged in a red frill, with three fresh mushrooms stuck on it every day, is bound to get people looking at them.

Last time Elvis H. went to school like that, the entire staff of teachers had heart attacks.

We hadn't been in the hall two seconds before Mr Millbank noticed him.

'Boy!' screamed Mr Millbank in Assembly. 'Get out here, boy!' and all the lads were nudging each other.

'Does he mean me?' they're going.

'Nah, he means thee,' they kept saying and in the end they pushed old Gary Smith the Dead Beat (from 'Elvis H. and the Dead Beats') out to the front.

'What do *you* want?' Mr Millbank snarls at Gary and Gary goes, 'Erm, erm, Sir.'

'Get out of the way, lad,' rasps Mr Millbank and roars down the hall and zooms to a halt in front of E.H.'s nose.

'You,' Mr M. goes, poke poke into E. Harris's chest. 'Out, lad. Out to the front.' And E.H. gets up and saunters down behind Mr Millbank, his three mushrooms just going a little bit brown at the edges.

'Back in your place, Pickle,' Miss Sanders says when I try and move down the lines to be alongside E.H. 'This is not Old Home week.'

She's somebody you have to watch, Miss Sanders. She only *looks* weak and ladylike. She's as tough as an old boot, really. A pair of old boots if it comes to that.

'Yers, Miss,' I tell her and bide my time.

Mr Millbank clomps up onto the stage and E. Harris goes up after him without a quiver. Luckily, E.H. is used to stages because of his rock group.

'They hold no fears for me,' he says and then the Head grabs him, turns and faces the school.

'This –' he shouts, nodding at E.H. who is wavering about on the end of his hand. 'This is a human being.'

There was total silence in the hall. You could have heard one of E.H.'s mushrooms

8

drop, it was that quiet.

'I know,' Mr Millbank goes on, 'that none of you believe it, but this is the truth I am telling you,' he roars. 'A human being, do you hear?'

Nod, nod, we all go.

'I,' Mr Millbank yells, 'am going personally to pick his mushrooms –' and then it sounded like a gale going backwards as everybody sucked in their breath.

''E's gonna pick his mushrooms,' Gary Smith drones aloud and Mr Millbank sent a look at him that should have burnt every last toenail off.

E. Harris pulled himself tall and straight. His face went pale and his Adam's apple bobbed up and down his neck like a yoyo because he was swallowing so hard.

'Then do it, Sir. Now, Sir,' he says and there's hardly a quiver in his voice at all.

'Yeah, do it!' Hoggy Morgan shouts, with his spots all over his face.

E. Harris looks at Hoggy and in a second, you could see wild horses fighting in the air. If anybody hates each other, it's Hoggy and E.H.

And then, in all that quiet, Mr Millbank picked E.H.'s three mushrooms and flung them down and stamped on them.

''E's gorn and stamped on 'is mushrooms,'

Gary Smith moaned sadly and Mr M. looked as if he were going to explode.

'Be quiet, Smith,' he fumed. 'Else I shall stamp on you!' and Gary opened his mouth to drone, 'E's gorna stamp on me' when he came to his senses and coughed instead.

'Right,' snaps Mr Millbank. 'Right.' And he glares at us all and then loosens his collar with one hand. 'Let this be a lesson to you all,' he goes on, squashing E.H.'s fungus underneath the soles of his shoes.

Squelch, it went.

'We shall now say our morning prayers,' Mr Millbank sizzled and bent his head and then snapped it up again and stared round the hall.

'Lower your heads, you heathens!' he roared and we all dropped our heads from our necks and then Mr M. starts, 'Our Father,' and we all went *drone*, 'Who art in heaven,' *drone*, when all of a sudden this little voice comes echoing down the hall.

''Scuse me,' it went, floating in the air and then standing still.

'God speaking,' comes this other voice right behind it.

'That ain't God,' says Hoggy Morgan.

'How dja know?' asks Mavis Jarvis.

Clip, goes Miss S. stalking round the hall like a tiger on her high heels, *clip*, straight round M. Jarvis's left ear.

'Desist, child,' Miss Sanders spits. 'We know it is not God, do we not, Morgan?' – *clip* round Hoggy's ear. 'Because God does not come from Workton and therefore God does not have a Workton accent. Right, Morgan?' – *clip*. 'Right, Jarvis?' – *clip, clip*.

'Arrrrrrh! I'm gonna tell me Mam of you,' whines old Mave.

''Scuse me,' this voice calls again. 'But I'm stuck –' And it went right up at the end and finished in a squeak. 'I'm stuck!' it went.

Mr Millbank kept right on praying.

'Thy will be done.'

'Fifty lines, Jarvis,' said Miss Sanders. ' "I shall tell my Mother about you." Right?'

'Right?' she went again when Mavis didn't answer.

'Yers, Miss,' grumbles old Mave.

''Ere, look, Lily.' Karen Green nudged me and I went peer upwards with just one eye – the other one was keeping a look-out for Miss S. – and there was this fellow, dangling with one hand from the outside of the window.

''E's lorst 'is ladder,' Karen whispers and M. Jarvis goes, 'Snerk, snerk, snerk. 'E's lorst more than his ladder. 'E's just lorst his grip!' and the next second, we heard this bang crash clatter.

There was nobody praying then, I can tell

you. Nobody even pretending to pray. We all opened both our eyes and stared up at the big window and there's the window cleaner with his bucket, swinging against the glass with his fingers scrabbling to get hold of anything they could grab, which wasn't a lot. Just bits of wood.

'He ain't got far to fall, that's one good thing,' Michelle Parrish says.

Smack goes the bucket against the window and a great long crack shoots up the glass.

''Elllllllllllllp! 'Elllllllllllllp!' we could hear this faint little voice crying.

'Amen,' roars Mr Millbank and we all go 'Amen' after him and then everybody starts talking at once.

'Silence!' Mr Millbank shouts. 'Rescue that man, Grey,' he tells Mr Grey, the sports teacher, and Mr Grey goes leaping off the stage, down the hall and straight outside.

'Hold on!' he's shouting. 'Help is at hand.'

''Elp!' comes this sad little voice again and then, zip, zip, went the window cleaner and vanished clean out of sight.

'He's gorn now, Sir,' Gary Smith cries. 'He's fallen down the window, Sir. Sir! Sir!'

'Smith,' Mr Millbank says tightly. 'Go, Smith, to my office and wait for me there.'

Poor old Gary shambles down the hall and then we saw Mr Grey's head go bob, bob past the bottoms of the windows.

'Too late,' droned Gary. ''E's gorn.'

Mr Millbank looked as if he was going to explode.

'Silence!' he roared. 'We shall carry on with morning assembly as if nothing had happened. Do you understand?' And everyone in the hall bellowed, 'YES, SIR.'

Mr Millbank let a quick grim smile flit on and off his thin lips.

'Right,' he said and swirled round in his black robe.

E. Harris was leaning against Mr Millbank's table, picking his teeth. He yawned just as Mr M. turned and looked at him.

Choke, goes Elvis, and snaps his mouth shut that fast, if he'd opened it again, all his teeth would have dropped onto the floor.

'Shut your mouth, Pickle,' Miss Sanders suddenly hisses, appearing like a genie out of a lamp. 'Try breathing through your nose as we all do. Ha!' she snapped and went prowling down the hall on her black high heels.

'Right, Harris,' Mr Millbank says very quietly. 'The next time you darken the doors of this school with mushrooms on your head will be the last time. Am I understood?' he roared.

'Yers,' E.H. says sadly.

'Yers . . . yes, what?' Mr M. snaps.

'Yers, Sir,' says E.H.

So, that was that and E. Harris got down off the stage and we sang 'Morning has Broken', which it certainly had, and then we were dismissed, just in time to see Mr Grey helping the window cleaner into school.

'And Harris,' shouts Mr M. 'Fetch a brush and shovel and sweep this disgusting mess up.'

'Me mushrooms, he means,' E.H. said drearily and I gave him one of my last mintoes.

'Thanks, Lil,' he says and then I wished I hadn't bothered.

'Daphne,' I tell him. 'Daphne.'

E.H. shrugged.

'Thanks, anyway,' he says and goes off kicking the floor.

'Feet up, up, up,' hisses Miss Sanders, right in his ear.

E.H. nearly jumped out of his skin.

'Hup. Hup!' repeats Miss S. and the last I saw of them, they were both going down the hall like bouncing balloons.

Chapter Two

The trouble with being my age is that nobody takes any notice of what you say at all.

'You always ignore me,' I tell my Mam and she looks round and goes, 'Who said that?'

They think they're so funny.

'When are you coming back home to live?' my Mam asks me and Mr Pickle, he who is my Dad, he sits bolt upright in the brown armchair and smirks, 'Come back home, Lilian. We love you and we want you here with us.'

I thought it was a speech he'd learnt to say off the telly.

'Your bedroom's there whenever you want,' my Mam says, who I am thinking about divorcing.

'Divorcing!' E.H. says when I tell him. 'You can't get a divorce from your parents, dumb cluck. It's only married people who do that.'

'Has anybody ever tried?' I ask him and he practises lifting one corner of his lip at me.

'This is my scornful look,' he says. 'What do you reckon? Be honest. Tell me the truth. I've got to get it right. It's going to come in handy, that look.'

I stared at E.H. who was standing there with one side of his mouth higher than the other.

'You remind me of somebody,' I tell him.

'John Lennon?' he says. 'Without hair. No? Well, erm, how about Rod Stewart? Without hair. No? Butch Cassidy? Little Richard, only bigger . . . ?'

'He's black,' I said.

'You can use your imagination, can't you?' E.H. returned smartly.

That made me blink a bit but I still shook my head.

'Got it!' Elvis snaps his fingers. 'It's the King, isn't it? The King himself, I remind you of? HRH Elvis Presley. Yesssss, well, I always knew it. *His* mouth went up at one side. I was given the right name, OK.'

I shook my head. Then it came to me.

'I know!' I shouted.

'Who? Who?'

'Stella's dog, Tiny,' I told him. 'Just before he licks you. You look like him.'

Well, that didn't go down very well but

E.H. really has a strong resemblance to Tiny when you look at him. With a bit of hair on his head, they'd pass for brothers.

'Ho, very funny,' E. Harris says wearily. 'There's always a joker in every pack.'

'Have they?' I ask him again when he'd calmed down.

'Have they what?'

'Has anybody tried to divorce their parents?'

'Nobody has ever tried to divorce their parents,' Elvis sighs. 'Because it cannot be done.'

'Perhaps I could set a fashion,' I say sourly but E.H. says you're stuck with the parents you get when you're born and that's all there is to it.

'But Mr Pickle left us when I was six,' I moan. 'That's nearly seven years ago. Why do I have to take him back now?'

'It ain't *you* taking him back, is it?' Elvis says. 'It's your Mam.'

All I can say is that it's not fair.

'You think you've got problems,' E.H. goes on. 'What about me? Huh? Huh?'

'What about you?' I snarl impatiently.

'What about my mushrooms? Gone – and I ain't got money for any more.'

'I thought you picked them off your bed-room wall,' I said because Rat Trap Flats are so damp, when they send the Rent men in, they're all equipped with machetes to hack their way through the undergrowth to people's purses.

'There's folk come into these flats,' Mr Kendal says. 'Who 'ave never been seen again. Lost, in a mighty wilderness,' and we stood and looked round all the concrete. 'One day they'll find their skeletons,' he went on. 'And that is all.'

Losing his mushrooms made E.H. slope around all day looking like a thunder cloud.

'It's not fair,' he tells Mr Kendal. 'What's wrong with mushrooms?'

'You're sick,' Mad Mave shouts. 'Sick, Harris. Whoever heard of anyone wearing mushrooms on their heads?' and she stomps about, purple as a bursting plum with rage.

Mr Kendal looks at E.H.'s green and red head and he frowns a bit and then he says 'But what do you wear them for, lad? I mean, why mushrooms?'

'Them's my, like, meaningful statement of life,' E. Harris tells Mr K. 'If yer see what I mean?'

Mr Kendal said as he didn't rightly see what he meant, no.

'Well,' E.H. starts. 'Mould, that's what mushrooms is, innit?' and Mr K nods. 'Well, then,' Elvis goes on. 'It stands to reason,

18

don't it? Mushrooms is my, like, personal statement about life, like, mushrooms is mould, the world is, like, mouldy, yeah?'

Mr Kendal thinks about this and then he starts to nod his head very slowly.

'Why,' he says. 'That is very good, Elvis,' and he looks at E.H. as if he's never seen him before. 'Very good indeed.'

This is exactly what E.H. is like. Brilliant.

My Gran says he'll go a long way in this life and she doesn't go on and say, 'And the further the better' like everyone else does.

'All the same,' she goes. 'I should get used to walking or riding in buses if I were you, Lily, if you're hitching your wagon to that lad's star.'

'I'm not riding on anybody's star, Gran,' I tell her, 'but my own.'

'That's exactly the right attitude, Lily,' she nods.

'Daphne,' I say and my Gran goes 'What? What?'

'Daphne,' I tell her. 'That's my new name.'

'I'm sure as I shan't call you Daphne,' my Gran snaps. 'Whatever next?' And she goes off muttering and moaning but why shouldn't I change my name?

Who wouldn't rather be called Daphne than Lily?

'One sees mud and one sees stars,' E.H.

says when I tell him and that's all I get out of him.

Mr Kendal told E.H. he was glad he'd told him (Mr Kendal) about his mould.

'I tell you why,' he says. 'Because I think I've got just the thing to cure it.'

'The only way to get rid of mould,' M. Jarvis says, butting in where she shouldn't be, as usual, 'is to kick it out, rip it off and then stamp on it. Yak. Yak. Yak.'

'Drop dead, Jarvis,' Elvis tells her but Mr K. rushes on, 'No, no. We don't want no dropping dead. We're getting a football team going. This afternoon. On the field. Two-o-clock. Be there. All of you!' and he waves a hand. 'We'll be new men when we've finished.'

'That should be interesting,' Karen Green yawns and picks a bit more nail polish off her nails. 'My Dad always wanted a lad, anyway.'

E.H. just went very pale. The only sport he has ever played in his entire life is marbles – and even then I always had to carry them for him.

That was when my Gran put me right.

'You give that lad his own marbles to carry,' she said. 'Just you remember this, my lass, for everything one person doesn't do, someone else has to do it for them and unless you've got a good excuse, what wants doing

20

for yourself, you do for yourself. One thing I can't abide is idleness.'

'Of course,' E.H. tells Mr K. quickly, 'I'll be glad to come and give you the benefit of my advice,' and Mr K. roared with laughter.

'You will have your little joke,' he says. 'Nay, no more talk of advice. It's legs I want there . . . and feet . . .'

Michelle Parrish did a hand stand on one hand and says to Mr Kendal idly through her upside down mouth, 'I'll be there, Mr K. You can rely on me.' And then she flipped over three times and vanished round a corner.

'That lass,' Mr Kendal mused. 'She's good enough to be on the telly. I wonder what the rules are about playing upside down?'

'You don't mean ter say the *lasses* are going to be in this 'ere team, Mr Kendal?' Hoggy Morgan said, all his words coming out like bus crashes, as usual.

'Certainly I mean to say the girls will be in the team,' Mr Kendal told him. 'Why, Mavis here has already volunteered to go in goal.'

'Grunt. Grunt,' says The Mouth and slaps her boyfriend on the back.

SMASH, her hand went and that made Hoggy draw his breath in sharply. If she'd done it to anybody else, they'd have been hurtled into the middle of next week.

'C,mon, cloth-head,' she simpers to

Hoggy. 'Me, you and your spots are going to practise.'

'Who could refuse an invitation like that?' Karen drawls and winks at me.

'And 'oo do you think you are, Miss High and Mighty?' Mavis snaps. 'You need to be cut down to size, you do,' and *clonk* she goes with one of her melon-sized fists, smack on top of Karen's head.

'Say your prayers, creep,' Karen grits. 'This is the end of your world.' And she goes for Mad Mave like a tornado.

'It ain't very ladylike to fight,' Mavis tells Karen as Karen goes smashing into her. 'Ooooof! Gerroff me!'

Karen's arms are going like pistons.

In, out, in, out, bash, bash, bash, they're going.

Old M.J. gets pretty tired of this and she grabs hold of Karen in a fury.

'Put her down!' Mr Kendal shouts. 'Put her down, I say. Dear heavens, put that girl down.'

'Yer don't know where she's bin,' chomps Hoggy slowly and then goes, 'Ha. Ha. Ha. That's a joke,' he tells us, as he looks at all our hatchet faces.

'It's you that's the joke,' Elvis snarls.

Mr Kendal tries to push in and grab Karen but Mad Mave has hold of her head and she's shouting, 'I'm going to play puzzles with you, Green. Where does a head go?' she shouts at the sky. Twist, crunch, she goes. 'Why – here,' and she refits Karen's head in a different place. 'Where does an arm go?' she asks the wall. Yank, twizzle. 'Why – here,' she says meanly.

'That'll do now,' Mr Kendal cries. 'That will just do.' But then Karen gets free and bang, crash, batter, she laces into Mavis.

M. Jarvis starts behaving like a mad bull who can't get out of a china shop. She manages to flatten everybody in a circle of three miles, including Mr Kendal, but not Karen, who's darting in and out like a hornet.

Jab, jab, jab, she's going.

'That's enough. That's just enough,' Mr Kendal roars, staggering to his feet. 'You'll not be in no goal, Mavis!' he bellows. 'And you, Karen. You won't even be in the team.'

'Don't wanna be in the team,' Karen grits out but then she grins and stops. 'All right then,' she says, beaming. 'All right. Seeing as how it's for you, Mr K. I'll stop hitting monkey muss here.'

And then Karen starts leaping up and down, crowing with joy.

'Hey, Hey, Hey!' she yodels. 'Just call me the greatest. I've beat 'er. I've beat 'er,' and she leaps up and down on the spot with her hands over her head clasped in a winner's salute.

'Yayyyyyyy!' she yells. 'Just call me Cassius Clay.'

Zonk, goes one of M.J.'s fists and poor old Karen staggers backwards, then flops onto the ground.

'Heh, Heh,' gloats M.J. 'And just call me Muhammad Ali.' And her and spotty Hoggy go off with their arms round each other, chortling and snurfling until the flats echoed with the noise.

'She ain't 'eard the last of this,' Karen sobs, when she can separate her mouth from her teeth again. 'You wait and see. I'll get even with her. Just see if I don't,' and then she collapses in tears.

'Dry yer eyes. Dry yer eyes,' Mr Kendal says. 'And let that be enough. I want no more such talk. None. None,' he goes on, raising his finger as Karen starts to speak again. 'If you ask me, it's about time we had a football team. What? What we need round here is some unity. Yers. Unity. And loyalty. And unity and loyalty is what we're going to have – if I have to tie you all to a football personally.' Snarl, he went, and stalked off with his football rule book in his hand.

'Now then,' he's muttering. 'Upside down players. What can the rules be there?'

'Unity and loyalty,' E.H. growls when Mr Kendal's disappeared. 'To what?'

'What?' says Gary the Dead Beat.

'Unity and loyalty,' Elvis repeats. 'To what? To this dump?' – and he flings his arm out. 'To a double bedstead?' And we all look at the double bedstead lying in the middle of the waste ground.

'Nah,' E. Harris goes on. 'I ain't playing no football because I ain't got no loyalty to this rubbish tip.' And we all stood looking at the concrete, wondering what to say next.

'Fans,' Gary Smith says suddenly and E.H.'s little ears pricked right up.

I could believe he used to be a dog once. No trouble at all.

'Fans,' E.H. repeats. 'Well, yes. There are my fans, of course. Yes. Yes,' he goes on. 'I can see that for the sake of my fans, I shall have to take part in Mr K.'s daft football team.'

He got out his comb to comb his hair. Swish, the comb goes and it makes E.H. yelp.

'I forgot for a minute,' he smirks. 'I ain't got no hair.'

'You ain't got no fans either,' I tell him but he just shrugs and says, 'You mustn't be jealous, Lily. Your turn will come. One day I might even ask you to marry me.'

'Well, I don't have to wait for one day to

tell you "No, thanks",' I say sharply but this just makes E.H. glint his teeth in my direction and smirk even more.

Miss Sanders isn't married but my Mam is and that's all I need to know for me to make my mind up.

Mr Pickle and his brown arm chair.

Huh!

Chapter Three

By two-o-clock there was me, Mr Kendal,
Alf on the wall, Stella Green and her dog Tiny
on the football field.

'That's it, then,' Mr K. shouts. 'I shall wash
my hands of the lot of you. If they can't be
bothered to turn up . . . well, that's it, then. I
shall wash my hands of the lot of you. If they
can't be bothered to turn up . . .'

'You've said that, Mr Kendal,' I tell him
because I could see us standing there till next
week and him still saying it.

'Said it! Said it! I should just think I 'ave
said it. What? There's no gratitude, that's
what it is. No gratitude. Here we are, with
my lovely football team, and where are they?
What? Where are they, eh? Not here. That's
where they are. Not here,' and Mr K. flings
his football down on the ground and dribbles
it to a clump of grass.

'Skill,' he goes on moodily. 'And talent.

Who cares?'

Well, me and Stella Green certainly didn't. We were so fed-up, we had to lean on each other just to stay on our feet.

'There'll be somebody here in a minute,' I tell Mr K. and he goes 'Humph!' and kicks the ball *whizz*, straight past Tiny's nose.

The next minute Tiny was playing dribbling with Mr Kendal and winning him.

'Dratted dog,' Mr Kendal roars. 'Come back here with that ball. Fetch that dog back, young Stella,' he orders and Stella shouts and shouts to Tiny until he eventually came back but he wouldn't let go of the ball. He laid down and draped a great long leg over it and showed his teeth every time Mr K. tried to get the ball back.

'Leave that dog at home in future,' he tells Stella, which is pretty much like telling Stella to leave her head at home next time she goes out.

'You want to be a mascot, don't you?' Mr K. asks furiously and Stella nods slowly, bends down, shakes Tiny's enormous paw and whips the ball out from under.

'Kill!' she says to Tiny, pointing at Mr Kendal and Tiny gets to his feet growling softly.

'STELLA!' Mr K. roars. 'Watch yourself, my lass,' and then young Stella gets Tiny to lie down again.

Stella doesn't like people very much.

'Entirely because she's been brought up with that daft dog,' my Gran says. 'She thinks dogs are better than people.' And then she swishes a duster over her sideboard and goes on, 'Not as I'm saying she's altogether wrong but, drat it all, the lass can't go to school with that walking shepherd's pie behind her.'

If it weren't for my Gran and E.H., I think I'd like dogs better than people as well.

'Might as well call it a day,' Mr Kendal says. 'Obviously no-one coming at all,' and just as he said that, three and a half thousand little lads poured onto the field through the top entrance.

'Heyup,' Mr K. said, all puzzled. 'Who's this lot?'

'We've come to play football, Mister,' they all started shouting and milled round him like water round a rock.

'Blow me,' Mr K. goes. 'There's some as got some sense, anyhow.' And he shouts his pal Alf, who is still sat on the wall, with his brown cigarette hanging out of the corner of his mouth.

'Alf!' he shouts. 'You tek this lot away and give 'em some practice.' And Alf drops off the wall and looks exactly like a garden gnome.

'Grunt,' he goes and then, 'Grunt. Grunt?' and Mr K. says 'Yers. Yers', impatiently and Alf and this tide of little lads flood the far side of the field.

And then everybody turned up at once. E.H., Deirdre Summers, Mavis Jarvis – and she's wearing a pair of purple stretch tights and an acid green jumper, which has E.H. covering his eyes and reaching for his sunglasses.

'You can take *them* off,' Mr K. orders straight away. 'There's no light now. What! Tha'll never see the ball, lad, let alone kick it.'

'Don't wanna see the ball,' E.H. moans but that leaves Mr K. cold.

Then there was Hoggy Morgan, Karen Green, Gary Smith, Michelle Parrish, Awful Warning (alias Peggy Lane alias Elizabeth Lane alias The Christmas Tree Fairy because normally she looks like one but not at the moment with her black and purple hair done in spikes and her circles of bright red on her cheeks and her eyes which can only open one centimetre due to her wearing three tins of mascara on them every time she moves out of their front door) and Awful Warning's boy-friend, Asquith.

'They've landed!' says Mr K. when he sees Peggy Lane and Asquith.

Then he looks at Peg's boyfriend.

'What's your name again?' he says.

'Asquith,' Asquith says. 'I ain't come to play, man. I've just come to watch.'

'No watchers,' Mr K. retorts smartly. 'You can be in the team, Asquith. I have great hopes for you. What? You've got a nice build for a footballer.'

'Hey, man,' Asquith says. 'I ain't taking off my chains.'

Asquith wears a chain across the back of his legs so he can't move very well and has to take little steps.

'I'm getting wise to this,' Mr K. says. 'Why the chains?' and Asquith swings his one long diamond earring and says 'Slavery, man. Free the pee-pull.'

'Free the who?' Mr Kendal asks.

'Pimples,' Mavis Jarvis shouts coarsely. 'Free the pimples and by the look of your phizogg, Squib, they need freeing. I ain't never seen such big pimples.'

Hohohaha, she goes.

Splat, goes Peggy Lane, and tries to haul Jarvis's toenails up through her throat.

'One more fight,' Mr K. says wearily, 'and that'll be it. Nothing for any of you.'

Asquith tossed his black and greeny-yellow spikes and dragged Awful Warning back.

M.J. stood there panting and Hoggy Morgan in his lace-up boots struts up to

Asquith and says, 'Kiss yer teef goodbye, pal. You've seen the last of them.'

'Get back into line,' Mr K. says. 'Back, back, back!' and he pushes and shoves at Hoggy until he's managed to move him over a blade of grass.

This Hoggy is like an out-of-work coal bunker. Moving him is as easy as moving a coal wagon with one finger.

'Wot's wiv your bald head, Elvis?' Asquith asks, looking all interested and Hoggy stamps back to his lady love, who slams his back with her great beefy hand.

'Great!' she smirks, fluttering her eyes. 'Killer.'

'Oooh!' Karen Green warbles. 'May hero!' and everybody falls about laughing save Mad Mave and Hoggy.

'Wot's wiv your bald head, Elv?' Asquith asks again and E.H. smoulders a bit and then points out there should be three mushrooms: '*In situ*,' he says, showing off.

'Hea-vee, man,' Asquith drawls and E.H. comes back smartly, 'Ain't heavy at all. It's hair that's heavy. Mushrooms is outré. Hair is antique. Even hair in spikes. Especially hair in spikes.'

'What?' says Asquith.

'Clank your chains, Asquith,' Elvis tells him. 'I ain't saying it again. Foreign language isn't like English, you know. You can't just go spreading that around as you wants.'

'When you've quite finished,' Mr K. breaks in. 'We've got about an hour to get this team together. Right,' he bellows. 'All line up.'

So, we all line up again and then Mr K. says 'Good. Good. Now, here's your places,' and he reels off a great list of Inside Lefts and Upside Downs.

'Sure thing,' Michelle says and walks up the field on her hands.

That left the rest of us in a quandary.

We all started milling about looking for somewhere to go out of the way.

'And where do you think you lot are going?' Mr Kendal howled as we traipsed up the field to lean on the goal posts.

'Come back. Come back. It's a laugh a minute with you lot. Get back 'ere,' so then we all traipsed back.

'Before we can start,' Mr Kendal says, 'we'd better find out if everybody knows what a football looks like.'

He held the ball up in the air.

'This is a ball,' he says. 'Right?' and we all nod, save Tiny. He leapt up and tried to drag it out of Mr K.'s hands.

'Down. Down!' Mr K. shouts. 'This ball goes bounce, bounce, when it hits the ground,' he goes on. 'But –' he pauses. 'But with our team, it ain't going to be long enough on the ground to bounce. Right?'

We all nodded again.

'You ain't allowed to touch the ball,' Mr K. says and beats Tiny's huge mouth of teeth off it. 'You ain't allowed to knock or pull each other to the ground – *you lot*,' he glared at everyone in turn. 'You ain't allowed to bash each other. Right?'

We nodded.

'Good,' he says. 'I shall now explain the rest of the game to you –' and off he went, rattle rattle rattle through all these rules and at the end he cries, 'Everybody got that?'

There was a stunned silence but Mr K. shouts 'Clear, everybody?'

'Clear as mud,' Karen Green mutters but Mr K. pretended not to hear her and hurries on to the next bit.

'Right,' he says. 'Now, before a match can start, a coin is tossed up into the air. Someone shouts 'Heads' and someone shouts 'Tails' and whoever wins gets to kick the ball first.'

Deirdre Summers yawned so wide, she almost fell down her own throat.

'Am I boring you?' Mr K. enquires.

'Yeah,' Deirdre says and takes out her triangle. *Ting*, she goes and then puts it away.

'Right,' Mr K. bustles on. 'Now for the coin. Then we'll get organised. We shall now throw the coin up in the air.'

I must say that seemed a very risky thing to me to do, given the lot that were standing there. E.H.'s sharp little eyes that had 'mush' in one and 'rooms' in the other. And Hoggy's face that had 'food' written all over it.

Still, Mr Kendal knew what he was doing.

'A coin. A coin,' he's mumbling and puts a hand in his trouser pocket. That comes out empty. Then he tries his coat pocket. Nothing there either. Then he shouts and asks Alf if he's got a coin.

'Grunt. Grunt?' questions Alf.

'Well, if you 'aven't, you 'aven't' Mr K. says irritably. 'Tut tut tut,' he's going. 'Useless. Utterly useless. Come on, you lot. One of you must have a coin,' but none of us had anything at all.

All we came up with were four buttons, two washers (from Awful Warning's necklace) and fourteen combs (E.H.).

'Well, I'll be danged' (!) Mr K. moans. 'Don't tell me we haven't got a single solitary coin.' Dead silence from everybody. 'Ain't we even got a foreign coin?' but there wasn't any kind of a coin anywhere.

'We're all right 'ere,' Mr Kendal says bitterly. 'Can't even start the dratted match without something to throw up in the air.'

'Try Mavis,' Karen suggests, but Mr Kendal

wouldn't listen to her. 'Throw her up in the air.'

'Very funny,' old M.J. snarls. 'You'll be laughing on the other side of your face yet, you will.'

'Drat and double drat,' Mr Kendal snaps and then he just happens to glance across the field and a worried look stretches right across his face.

'Here,' he says sharply. 'Who's that lot?' and we all turn round for a look and there's all these lads and lasses in black and white uniforms pouring onto the field.

They were like treacle coming out of a tin. They poured through the gate in the wall, over the grass and straight on to the pitch.

'Yerk,' Deirdre Summers shrills. 'Yerk. Yerk. What are they? Large ants?'

In front of all these lasses and lads was a tall thin man who looked exactly like an Admiral with his uniform and his braid and his white bits and gold bits and his hat.

'Who're you?' Mr Kendal demands. 'Who are you lot?'

'St. John's,' this man says smartly, 'Ambulance Brigade at your service' and he winks and nods and touches his hat at Mr Kendal.

'But what are you doing here?' Mr Kendal asks.

'Practice' the S.J. man says. 'Heard as you was starting a new football team. No man is an island. My new recruits behind me,' he nods and tucks and all these kids behind him clutch their bandages and look for somebody to flatten on a stretcher.

'Well, all right, but tha' must keep out of the way,' Mr Kendal says nervously and looks all uneasy.

One of these S.J. kids tumbles over Michelle high-kellying in the grass and they have to put splints on both his arms to stop him smothering Michelle feet to forehead in bandages.

'Gerroff me. Gerroff me!' poor old Michelle kept yelping. 'I'm not hurt. I was high-kellying. Mr Kendal! Gerremofferme!'

'She's one of my football team,' Mr Kendal shouts. 'Leave the lass alone and take them bandages off her. She's got to kick a ball.'

'Sorry, sorry, *sorry*!' says the Admiral. 'Just a touch of over-enthusiasm.'

'I'll smash 'em inter little pieces if they come near me,' Mavis J. growls and three quarters of the Ambulance Brigade fainted clean away with shock at hearing a real orang-outang speak.

'Ha!' Mr K. says suddenly. 'There is something you can do.'

'Why, anything,' the Admiral says, smiling

like mad.

'You could lend us a tenpenny piece to get this dratted game going,' Mr K. says hopefully and the Ambulance man nodded.

'Why, yes, of course. My pleasure.' So he felt in his pocket and fished out a fifty pence piece.

'Will this do?' he says. 'I don't seem to have any less,' and I could almost hear everybody's brains whizzing round and clanking at the sight of a fifty pence piece.

'That's fine. Fine,' Mr Kendal says impatiently and whips this coin out of the Admiral's hand.

'Right, you lot,' he shouts. 'Football team ready!' and he flips the coin up in the air.

Twirling and whirling it went up and up.

'Heads or tails?' Mr K. roared.

'Heads!' shouts Mad Mave.

'Tails!' shouts Deirdre Summers.

'Hot dogs!' shouts Hoggy.

'Mushrooms!' shouts Elvis Harris.

The next second, poor old Mr K. vanishes under a pile of bodies, all scrambling to get their hands on this fifty penny piece.

'Could have told you that would happen,' I said to Mr Kendal after we'd pulled him out from the bottom of the pile and straightened him up.

'That man there,' shouts the S.J. man. 'A

casualty.'

'Aaaagh!' screams Mr K. as he looks up just in time to see a black wave of these S.J. kids surging up and over him again.

'By gum,' he shouts through a mouthful of mud, dragging himself upright. 'Would you credit it? Dun't tha know enough to stop, you kids, when somebody's standing in thy way?'

Zoom, a stretcher appears like a big white moth and Mr K. very nearly vanishes on it.

'Darn it!' he's shouting at these uniforms. 'Darn it. I'm all right. I'm all right, I tell you,' and a hundred kids scowl at him and mutter and roll up their stretcher and take it away again.

'Sorry,' says the S.J. man. 'A little bit too keen but,' he laughs, 'very understandably so. I mean – a football match – the atmosphere – the excitement.'

'Atmosphere! Excitement!' Mr K. repeats bitterly, and we all stare round the pitch black field.

It had started to rain and now it was coming down in concrete lamp standards. You could have swum off that field without any bother at all.

'What you needs is a dock leaf,' Deirdre hums.

'To put over your head,' she added hurriedly when Mr Kendal looked as if he was going to cry.

'What we need is a new football,' Mr K. sobbed, dragging this poor little screwed up bit of leather out of Tiny's jaws.

'Couldn't you have kept an eye on it?' he asks the fresh air. 'Right. Right. That's it. I'm calling it a day. We 'asn't even kicked the ball and 'ere it is, ball bust, dark fallen, team beaten. That's the end, I tell you. The living end,' and he clumps away across the grass.

'Ah! Ah, ha!' the Admiral peeps, all polite and nice. 'Oversight,' and he chuckles. 'My coin. Fifty pence piece?'

'Give it 'im back,' Mr Kendal roars, without turning round. 'Whoever's got it, give it 'im back.'

No-one moved and Mr Kendal glanced over his shoulder.

'No fifty pence piece,' he says. 'No nothing. I shall wash my hands of the lot of you. I shall. Without a doubt. The lot of you.'

'Why, it ain't come down yet, look,' Massive Mave shouts at the Admiral, pointing in the sky.

Just as he looks up, the fifty pence piece clonks him straight on the forehead.

'Aaaagh!' he goes. 'My head. My head!' and the next we saw of him, he looked as if he were wearing a turban, he had so many bandages wrapped round his poor old poll.

'That's it, then,' Mr K. says. 'We'll meet next week.' And he started walking off the field again.

''Oo knows?' he says bleakly. 'We might even get to kick a ball. Always supposing,' he goes on, 'we manage to get a new ball.' Trudge, trudge.

'Mr Kendal,' M. Jarvis cries. 'Oh, Mr Kendal. Can I be the goalie, can I?'

'You can be the *goal*, if you want,' Peggy Lane sneers. 'Your mouth's big enough.'

'And your mouth's big enough to get you into trouble,' Mave says meanly. 'If you don't watch it, I'll use you as the ball.'

'You and whose army?' Awful Warning shouts, her black mascara falling in torrents down her cheeks.

'I don't need no army to sort you out, punk,' M.J. retorts.

'That'll do!' Mr K. roars back.

'Can I, Mr Kendal? Can I be the goalie next week?' M.J. whines. 'Please, Mr Kendal. Please can I be the goalie? Can I?'

'Yers,' Mr Kendal snarls at last and splashes a bit further up the field.

'Hurray. Hurray. Hurray!' old Jarvis carolled, skipping like a herd of elephants across the mud to the goal post. 'I am the goalie,' she goes, simper, simper. 'Look at little me, being the goalie. Look at what I can do.' And she leaps up in the air, grabs the cross-bar of the goal and starts swinging on it like a gorilla.

'Look at me,' she cried. 'Look at me!' And the Admiral had to order all his kids to look up in their First Aid books, 'Wild Animals and How to Treat Them.'

'It's there somewhere,' he shouts and they all peer narrow-eyed at Mad Mave.

The next second, there was a great cracking noise and M.J. smacks on to the ground, her giant hands still clutching the whole of the cross-bar which had broken under her weight.

Awful Warning fell flat on her face laughing.

'Mr Kendal,' Mavis Jarvis shouts in a whisper. 'Erm, Mr Kendal . . .' and when he turned round, rain pouring off his flat cap, she said, 'You know when we get that new ball, Mr Kendal, well, can we get a new goal post as well?'

Chapter Four

It was pouring rain this morning, inside and outside the school. Miss Sanders was in a mad mood and she was slinking up and down the classroom, spitting with fury the whole entire morning.

Sftt, she goes. 'Homework?' and everybody starts scrabbling about in their bags looking for their books.

E.H. gets his out and Miss S. opens it and goes *sftt*, *sftt* again and then she reads out what's in E.H.'s book.

'10p Each Way "Roaring River" 2.00 Haydock Park.'

'The meaning of this?' Miss Sanders growls. 'The meaning, boy?'

'It's a bet, Miss,' E.H. starts. 'You see, you puts ten p. . . . .' and Miss Sanders nearly decapitates him.

Sftt. *Sftt*. *Sftt* she rages. 'Hundred lines, Harris. "I must not gamble."'

'But ...' E.H. goes.

'Two hundred,' Miss Sanders snips, her lips as tight as wire.

E.H. opened his mouth and Miss S. stood waiting to pounce on the words as they came out but E.H. went 'Herf Herf,' instead and Miss S. had to prowl away.

'Forgot mine, Miss,' Michelle Parrish says, picking her purple nail varnish off in front of Miss Sanders' 'very eyes,' as Miss S. screamed.

Sftt. Sftt goes Miss S. and removes old Michelle from her chair in one go.

'Purple, Parrish?' she says. 'Purple polish, you disgusting child? Yuk. Yuk. Parrish. Why not pale pink?'

Then it was our turn to go 'Yuk Yuk.'

Not as that bothered Miss Sanders. Her skin's so thick, you could bounce bullets off it.

'Out to the washroom. Scrub those nails, Parrish, double quick,' Miss Sanders steams. *Sftt. Sftt.*

'Miss,' old Michelle says wearily and staggers out of the room.

'Shan't see her again till tomorrow morning,' Karen mutters and Miss S. whirls round.

'Interesting conversation, Green?' she asks and Karen shakes her head and says 'No, Miss. Boring, Miss, really.'

Sftt, says Miss Sanders and then she suddenly snaps, 'Carol Service!' and everybody looks round for this new lass.

'Never saw 'er,' Gary drones.

'Dumb name, Carol,' M.J. sniggers.

'She can sit next to me, Miss,' Hoggy says and snurfs, until old M.J. reaches over the thirty-six desks between them and practically pins his whole body onto the end of a ruler.

'Scream,' goes Hoggy.

'Who can? Who can?' Miss Sanders bites out.

'Carol Service,' Hoggy moans, this ruler almost sticking out of his back. 'She can sit next to me,' he storms, staring at M. Jarvis and making a face.

Well, we think he was making a face.

Sftt hisses Miss Sanders. 'Stupid boy. No such person. CAROL SERVICE,' she bellows. 'For Christmas Assembly.' *Sftt* – and then we knew why she was so mad.

One minute there was thirty-four real live people in that room, the next there was thirty-four dummies.

'I want volunteers,' Miss Sanders dripped meanly and when nobody put their hand up, she says 'Ho. *Sftt* – Very well, children. You, you and you. And you, you and you. Then you, you and you and let me see, ah yes, this immensely tall thin and disgusting person hiding under her desk: (me) *you*.' And by that time, she's covered everybody in the blinking class.

'Can't sing, Miss,' drones old Gary the Dead Beat.

'I know that,' Miss S. says sharply. 'None better, Smith. Close your mouth and breathe through your nose. In, out. In, out.' Then all that seemed to put her in a really good mood.

It was us that was going *Sftt! Sftt!* then but did Miss Sanders care? Huh! Did she Hector.

'Voluntary Rehearsal tonight,' Miss Sanders says cheerfully. 'And I shall expect everyone to be there. Those that are not will live to regret the day. Clear?'

There was a dead silence.

'Clear?' she cried again.

'Yes, Miss,' we all say and that's that for the day.

'How can it be voluntary?' Karen moans. 'When Miss Sanders threatens to half murder you if you don't turn up?'

But this is not one of those questions that want an answer and we all trail home muttering 'Good King Wenceslas' under our breath ready for the night.

If I'd known Mr Pickle was waiting for me, I'd have been humming a different tune altogether.

'Here's your Dad,' my Gran says, when I get in and throw my coat on the sofa. 'And pick that coat up and put it away properly. Coats don't grow on trees.'

'Hello, Lily,' Mr Pickle said, all smiles and honey.

'Daphne,' I told him. 'D.A.P.H.N.E.'

'What?' he said.

'Take no notice of her,' my Gran snaps. 'She's getting to be a right little Madam. Daphne indeed. This is her idea of a new name, you know.'

'Oh,' says Mr Pickle. 'Oh, well, in that case, shall I call you Daphne?' he asks me.

That nearly sent me for six, I can tell you, but I wouldn't let *him* know it.

'Please yerself,' I said and Mr Pickle starts again 'Well, Daphne. I've come to ask if you want to come home and live with me and your mother.'

'I haven't got a mother.'

'That'll do,' my Gran says sharply. 'Haven't got a mother indeed. Why, you've got a perfectly good mother. I don't know what's come over you lately, my girl.'

'I don't want to go home,' I say and Mr Pickle looks down at his shoes and picks thirty-nine invisible hairs off his jeans.

'Look,' he says, 'I know we don't know each other very well, but I do want to start again, Lily. Tell you what,' he goes on. 'Why don't you think about it. Think about coming home for Christmas. Think about having Christmas with your own Mam and Dad.'

'Yerk,' I said.

'Just think about it,' Mr P. rushes on. 'That's all I'm asking. That's not asking too much, is it?'

'Yes,' I tell him because already this thinking is like a prickly burr in my mind. 'It is too much to ask.'

'She'll think about it,' my Gran says smartly. 'And if she doesn't, I shall want to know why.'

That seemed to be that. I never got a chance to tell Mr Pickle that I was thinking about a divorce from him and my Mam. I never got chance to say I'd rather be eaten by wild dogs – 'Never heard anything like it' (Gran) – than live with my Mum and him.

'You've got altogether too much to say, my lass,' my Gran tells me when Mr Pickle has sloped off through the door, knocking over her little table with the china dish on it, scuffing his shoe against the white paintwork and leaving a great big black mark and tripping over her red rug which lies in front of the door.

'He was always what you would call an awkward man, your Dad,' she says to me irritably, picking up the pieces of her dish and rubbing at the black mark on her paintwork.

'Why your Mam couldn't have married somebody else, I'll never know.'

'I don't know why she had to get married in the first place,' I tell her but my Gran just swipes at me with her cloth and raps, 'Go and get your tea. There's hardly time to breathe in this house before something else wants doing.' Then I really felt homesick. I hate being snapped at.

Before Mr Pickle rolled up like a bad penny, my Mum and me used to watch television till midnight sometimes and when she was working on afternoon shift, I'd get my tea ready and her supper and we'd pad about for an hour before it was time for bed.

'I'm sorry I snapped at you,' my Gran said and gives me a hug. 'Look, you nip down to the shop and buy us a cream bun. I think we've earned a little treat.'

All the same, I see I've started thinking about my Mam and Mr Pickle and being at home at Christmas.

With a bit of luck, they'll have split up again by then.

It wasn't a bit of luck we needed for the Carol rehearsal. It was two ton.

When we trailed into the hall, Miss Sanders had a long bench lined up on the stage.

'Right!' she shouts and she can certainly shout.

'What!' says Karen. 'She don't behave like no woman teacher. She ought to be wearing big black boots and a red handkerchief around her neck, the way she shouts.'

'Right,' bellows Miss S. 'On the back row, standing on the bench that you will readily see is there . . .' Pause. 'Will be the angels.'

That led to a stampede, you may be sure. Elvis Harris nearly grew some hair in the rush for the door, he was moving that fast.

'Back,' roars Miss S. 'Back, I say,' and she beats everybody round the head with her carol book until we were back inside.

'Snerkle, snurf, ug, goomph, glup?' simpers old M.J. 'Miss?'

'Where did we go wrong, Jarvis?' Miss Sanders asks, and you can almost see flakes of frost coming out of her mouth, she's so icy and cold. 'The education system has failed you, child. Years at school and still unable to *articulate*.' She raps M.J. smartly on the head. 'Try again.'

'Please, Miss. Can I be an angel, Miss?' old Mave coos.

'There ain't no huge enormous angels, Jarvis,' Karen shouts. ''Cos there ain't wings big enough to carry them, see?' and she shouts with laughter. The only one who does, I might add, with Miss S. looking at her like an iceberg.

'Silence, Green,' Miss Sanders snips. '*You* can be an angel as you know so much about them. And *wings*, child,' she snaps. 'Large white wings made of cardboard and foil. By you. In the hours of darkness when lessons are finished.'

'But, *Miss*,' wails old Karen and behind her, Mad Mave seethes and burns with fury.

'You can be something else, Jarvis,' Miss S. says.

'A donkey!' shouts Karen and gets fifty lines:
'Being coarse doesn't make one hoarse,
But always makes one a donkey.'

That settled old Karen's hash. She said it would take her a week to work out what she's got to write, never mind actually writing it.

'Heh. Heh. Heh,' Mavis J. goes and Miss Sanders tells her she can be a wise man.

'With a dark grey blanket, Jarvis,' she says. 'On your head a twist of black string over a striped tea towel. We shall say no more about your costume, Jarvis, but instead shall expect to see it next Monday night.'

Miss Sanders makes everybody very, very tired. *She* doesn't get tired, though. Oh no, not her. She just goes on and on for ever in her black high heels and her long skirts.

'We shall have a back row of angels, a second standing row of lesser beings, say . . .

shepherds and so forth, three wise men kneeling on the front row together with, oh . . . citizens, I think. Yes, citizens. All clear? Right. Now to practise. On the back row, up on this form, will be you, you, you and you.'

Miss S. picks out seven and they all traipse up on to the stage and climb up onto this form.

'You can be the centre angel, Karen,' Miss Sanders tells her and Karen grumbles and groans her way into the middle, knocking poor old Gary Smith clean out of the way with her sharp elbows and stamping feet.

'Watch it, Green,' Gary says but this Karen, although she doesn't look it, she's a lot tougher even than Awful Warning, who gets to be a citizen, kneeling on the first row.

'Move her out of the way, Miss,' Deirdre Summers mutters. 'One of her spikes is going up me nose.'

'Then move your nose, Summers,' Miss S. snaps. 'Move your nose, child.'

'I'll move it, Miss,' Mavis Jarvis offers. 'Let me move it.'

'Desist,' Miss Sanders says simply. 'Desist and open your carol books.'

Everybody moans and groans and mutters and finally gets their carol books open. Mavis J. lets hers drop over E.H.'s face, who just happens to be kneeling in front of her, and he knocks this book in the air and leans on M.J.'s toes.

'Oh. Oh,' she cries. 'He's hurt my toes, Miss. Miss! Miss!'

'That will *do*,' Miss Sanders says.

'I'll have to go and look at me toes, Miss,' old Mave carries on. 'Oh, oh, he's really 'urt them, Miss. I thinks they're bleeding.'

'Go! Go! Go! Go!' Miss Sanders roars. 'Now, you lot,' and we all jerk to attention, which causes Karen to fall off the bench on top of Hoggy Morgan.

'Here, you leave my boyfriend alone,' M.J. shouts and Karen flicks her fingers.

'I wouldn't touch him with a barge pole,' she says and Hoggy and his pimples all stare at Karen as if she's a sausage roll.

M.J. and her toes go limping out through the side of the curtain and Miss Sanders says to Miss Michaels on the piano, '"Angels from the Realms of Glory", please, Miss Michaels.'

Miss Michaels goes beam, presses a piano key and then Miss S. taps her stand.

'One. Two. Three. Now!' she yells, and we all start singing 'Angels from the Realms of Glory'.

'Good. Good,' roars Miss S.

'Wing yer flight o'er all the earth,' we bellow and the next second, the entire back row of angels vanished.

'What?' questions Miss S. looking at this suddenly empty space where seven angels had been.

Miss Michaels' hands froze on the piano keys and all you could see were her eyes, peering over the top of the piano.

'Ye who . . .' she plays and stops.

'Where've they gone?' she asks. 'Where are the angels?'

'We're 'ere,' cries Karen Green. 'We're 'ere –' and she and the other six angels stagger to their feet and totter forward.

'Honk, honk, honk,' goes old M.J. from behind the stage curtain. 'Honk, honk, honk. That'll teach you to cross me, Green,' she sniggers and goes on, 'Oh dear. Oh deary me. Did the nice little bench tip over then? Heh, heh, heh.'

'One minute it was there, the next it had gone,' Gary hums sadly. 'Gone, right from under our feet –' and all we could hear then were the angels chasing Mavis J. the Wild Man of Borneo.

'Didn't he have a bone through his nose?' asks Gary.

'I should think Karen'll see to that,' drawls Awful Warning, dusting down her plastic bin liner skirt and silver mesh stockings.

'I'll kill 'er. I'll kill 'er!' we could hear Karen half sobbing.

Miss Sanders sighed, threw her little conductor's stick down and then said, 'This job will be the end of me. What in the world made me think I wanted to do it? Why? Why?' she asks Miss Michaels but Miss M. is still trying to work out what happened to the angels in the first place.

So, that was the end of that rehearsal.

It's going to be some Christmas, I can see that a mile away.

Chapter Five

There was a good bit of excitement last night outside number three flats.

Windsor House is what they're really called and my Gran says whoever gave them that name has a real sense of humour.

'My word,' she says. 'They must have died laughing over their name boards. You can just picture the Queen Mother coming out of there in powder blue, now can't you?'

When everybody gets together in the flats, it looks as if there's been a funeral because they all wear dark colours.

'There *as* been a funeral,' E.H. says darkly. 'They're in mourning for their lives.'

If my Gran had shot up any straighter, when she heard this, she'd have turned into a ruler.

'They're what?' she asks, staring hard at Elvis.

'In mourning for their lives,' Elvis says

again. 'For what might have been.'

'My word, but you're a clever lad,' my Gran says and looks at E.H. as if he's got two heads. 'Where do you get it from?' she asks. 'Go on, you can tell me.'

Smirk, goes E.H. and fishes out of his pocket this old battered book.

'Some out of 'ere,' he points at the book. 'And the rest out of here' he points at his head with its three mushrooms glued on.

'I'll accept the first one,' my Gran tells him but says she has severe doubts about the second.

'That's because you're prejudiced,' E.H. says smartly. 'Because you don't expect me to have any brains. If I was on telly . . .' but my Gran wasn't listening.

'See?' Elvis tells me. 'They don't want to hear the truth.' And he gets his comb out to comb his hair.

'You haven't got any hair,' I remind him and he sighs and puts his comb away.

'There's a high price to pay for principle,' he moans. 'No hair. No comb.' And he shuffles about and kicks the concrete.

'Don't you be late out, Lily,' my Gran shouts and hurries up the stairs to her flat.

'What about this 'ere bonfire?' E.H. asks and just then, Mr Kendal comes zipping round the corner.

Since he's started the football team, he doesn't walk anywhere any more. He jogs, hops, runs, leaps, sidles, dances, skips. Everything but walk. Keeping up with him is like keeping up with a kangaroo.

'Nice night, Mr K.,' you say and he goes, 'Yers –' leap, land – 'It is –' hop, dance, sidle. 'Very nice –' and then he swirls round a corner and leaves you staring into thin air.

'That there bonfire ain't anywhere near big enough,' he shouts now. 'I'm asking everybody to come out and collect for it. We'll charge twenty pence and put it to football funds. Right? Right. Fish 'em all out.'

And he was gone.

By the time we'd raked up all the kids, he was back.

'We'll divide the flats into quarters,' he says. 'You lot take that bit,' and he points to Gary Smith's team. 'And you lot, that bit,' and Hoggy Morgan goes grunt, grunt. 'That bit you lot can have,' and off shuffles Awful Warning and Asquith with his chains. 'We'll take Windsor House,' he tells me, E.H., Karen, Stella Green and Tiny, Deirdre Summers and Mavis Jarvis, although what she was doing a half a centimetre away from Hoggy, I do not know.

'Follow me!' Mr Kendal shouts and we all trail after him.

We go down the first garden path to the front door and E.H. steps into the grass and is lost for ever.

'Keep to the path,' Mr K. yells. 'This garden ain't been tended to since it was a field.'

'Erm . . . Mr K.,' I start, when there's this terrible racket coming out of the grass and the bushes and the seventeen bashed-up cars lying there – and E.H. suddenly leaps out in front of Mr K., shortening his life for ever, Mr Kendal tells him.

'By ga, lad,' he puffs. 'Tha's took years off my life. What? Jumping out of yon jungle like that.'

'I'll thank thee to keep thy opinions to thyself,' comes this voice from the front door. 'This is what is called a natural garden.' And Mr Franklyn peers out into the dark and shouts, 'Put that chicken back wheer tha found it, youth.'

'Chicken?' E.H. says. 'I thought it were a duck.' And this white thing in his hands is going chunter, chunter, peck, peck, as viciously as it knows how.

'It might be a duck,' Mr Franklyn shouts. 'It could well be a duck but it ain't being a duck whilst it's in your hands, now is it? Put it down.'

Elvis put this duck down and it went waddling down the path moaning and groaning and complaining like mad.

'Friend of the family, is that duck,' Mr Franklyn says and swoops it up into his arms.

'Well, well. That is . . . we're collecting for the bonfire,' Mr Kendal says finally and Mr Franklyn plays his torch around his garden.

'I'd like to help,' he starts. 'But as you can see, I haven't nothing to give you.' And he switches his torch off and goes back inside.

'What about this ratty old three piece suite?' Mr Kendal shouts through the letter box.

Mr Franklyn steams out again and stomps up to his three piece suite and tests the material. It's as wet as anything and there's a thick veil of frost on it.

'Hmmmmmm,' he says and then looks at us. 'You can have it for ten pence,' he says slyly and Mr Kendal snorts 'Ten pence! Ten pence! Why, you stingy old devil. I'd want paying to tek it away.' And he marches us all back down the path.

'Single file, you lot,' he cries and just then, there's this terrible quacking and barking and furious noise and old Tiny comes out through the grass bottom first, tail up in the air and when he whips round to face us – there, in his muzzle, is the duck.

'Quack!' this duck goes and Stella pounces on Tiny and starts bashing him with her little hands.

'Drop that duck,' she's yelling. 'Drop that duck!'

'Friend of the family,' roars Mr Franklyn and races back to the house to fetch an axe with which he is going to chop Tiny's head completely off his shoulders.

'Completely,' he screams and we all start bashing Tiny then.

'Drop it!' Mr Kendal tells him and we can hear Mr Franklyn opening and shutting drawers and then he shouts 'Hah! Got it!'

'He's coming, Mr Kendal!' young Stella quivers and starts to cry.

Tiny looks up at us all, this duck squawking in his huge mouth.

'Quaaaak. Quaaaaak!' it's going.

'DROP!' Mr Kendal shouts at the top of his voice and Tiny opens his mouth and the duck flops onto the floor and bustles away, all feathers and noise.

Without another word, Mr K. hurries us all down to the gate and through it and we gallop smartly down that street with Mr Franklyn shouting behind us, 'If there's one feather missing, I'm coming to get yer.'

Tiny went around for the rest of the night with his muzzle linted with duck feathers and frost that had slid off the grass onto his nose.

'Best get rid of them feathers,' Mr K. said

but Tiny wouldn't let anybody brush his nose so they stopped where they were. No-one fancied being sucked straight down Tiny's throat at all.

'Father Christmas ain't in it,' Mr K. said irritably and wondered if dogs – and come to that, kids – were worth the trouble.

'I wouldn't know how to answer that,' he rumbles on. 'Absolute *reign of terror* from both. Shouldn't be allowed.'

There wasn't a lot of talk after that for a bit. Everybody was exhausted and we all trailed from door to door dead quiet but we began to cheer up when we saw how much stuff we were beginning to get together.

'Right,' says Mr K. 'That'll do for the flats. Now for the houses.'

We turned into Gorse Street and Deirdre Summers knocked on the first door.

'Have you got anything for the bonfire, Missis?' she asked this woman who came to the door and this woman says smartly 'Yers, I have, now you comes to mention it. *Jack!*' she shouts and out ambles this chap who stands blinking in the light.

'Take him,' she tells Deirdre with a jerk of her head and then she vanishes back down the hall.

'Erhum,' Deirdre coughs, tings her triangle and backs off down the yard. 'Sorry,' she says and this bloke slams the door and the last we hear, he's shouting 'Betty. Betty. What did you mean by that, Betty?'

I knocked on the next house and this chap almost cheered when I told him what I'd come for.

'Why,' he says. 'You've come to the right house, my girl. Down that garden there's an old shed. It's dropping down. Time it was gone. You can have that.'

He points down this long thin garden.

'It's at the bottom. You can take it through the gate and out round the back. Dost tha want me to show it you? You can't miss it.'

'We'll manage, Mister,' E.H. pipes up and Mavis goes galumphing down this chap's path at a hundred miles a minute.

'Found it!' she shouts back and this man goes, 'Football's on. I'll leave you to it then.' And he shuts the door and we all totter down his pitch black garden.

'Might have left a light on,' Karen grumbles and Tiny flashes past us, pulling Stella behind him.

'Where's Mr Kendal?' Karen asks and it turns out he's with old Deirdre at the next house.

'Shall I fetch him?' But E.H. says there is no need at all to fetch Mr K. *He* can handle the shed and anything else, come to that.

'My He Man,' Karen says in that wiped-out voice she uses for lads.

'I've got my night eyes now,' E.H. says and tells us to let him through. 'It'll only take me a minute to work this out.'

It took him less than that because no sooner were we near this shed, than it got up and started to walk away from us.

'Heyup,' E. Harris says. 'Where's it going?'

The shed suddenly plonked onto the ground and M. Jarvis flung one of its windows open and shouts out, 'C'mon, you lot. Let's get this shed out of here.'

E. Harris sighed and started ordering everybody about. 'You go there and you there and you somewhere else,' and old Mavis got so fed up of waiting that she and the shed were trundling off at a rate of knots down the garden before any of us managed to get inside it.

'You can stop out there, Lily –'

'*Daphne*,' I muttered but E.H. swept on, '– and tell us where we're going.' Then his head vanished back through the window and the shed went careering off.

Smack, it went and there were all bumps and shouts and cries coming out of it.

Up goes the window again.

'What were that?' E.H. demands. 'Now,

what were that? I thought I told you to tell us where we're going?' he grinds out.

'You never gave me chance to get in front of you,' I tell him. 'And if you want to know what that was, it was the garden gate.'

'Then open it, nitwit,' grotty E.H. shouts. 'Open the gate.'

'Open it yourself,' I snap back, really fed up with the lot of them.

'Now, come on,' E.H. says. 'Get the gate open and give us directions . . . Daphne,' he chokes, so that cheered me up a bit and I nipped forward, opened the gate for them and shouted, 'Straight on.'

The window slammed shut, the shed teetered about a bit and then it swung over to one side.

'*Straight on*,' I yelled and they straightened up.

'Turn right. TURN RIGHT!' I shouted and the shed turned right and straight down the alley.

'Left,' I said to the shed window. 'LEFT!' I bellowed as the shed went straight on.

I was beginning to feel a bit breathless by this time and we'd reached the road.

'Halt,' I called out. 'HALT, HALT, HALT!' I screamed as the shed looked as if it was going to surge across the road in front of a giant lorry.

The shed stopped suddenly at the side of the road, bangings and crashings coming from inside it. I leant against its side quivering. I could almost see the headlines in the paper, *KIDS CRUSHED IN SHED*.

I pushed the window up and said to E.H., 'I'm going to stand in the middle of the road.'

'Best place for yer,' E.H. says, snerk snerk.

'I'm going to stand in the middle of the road and direct you across,' I shouted at them. 'You was nearly run over then.'

I crashed the window down and went and stood in the middle of the road with both my arms stretched out.

'MOVE!' I roared at the top of my voice and the shed went bump, bump, bump, off the edge of the pavement.

'Gerrofferme shoe,' I could hear Karen whimpering.

'Would somebody get that dog's tail out of my ear?' M.J. was grumbling and then old Tiny started barking and the shed rocked into the middle of the road just as a car came screaming round the corner.

I whipped round and yelled, 'STOP. STOP. SHED CROSSING', at the top of my voice and this car screeches to a halt and a bloke leaps out of it and reels back when he looks behind me.

'I don't believe it,' he says. 'Crystal.

Crystal,' (!) he cries. 'I've gone blind!' And Crystal gets out of the car and she goes, 'Myyyyy heavens. What's that?' and she's pointing to the bottom of the shed.

I turn round with her to have a look and all me and Crystal and the blind man can see is this shed and a row of feet at the bottom of it.

The blind man bends down and he says, 'I don't believe this. I don't believe it. I'm dreaming. What's them?' he asks Crystal and she bends down and says 'Myyyyy heavens. There's four paws there as well,' and they look at each other as if the world's just ended.

Flomp, goes the shed and crashes to the ground and then there's this unearthly silence.

'Stand back, Crystal,' this man says and Crystal is starting to giggle.

I think to myself she's probably been having a drink.

Then the car man walks up to the shed and hammers on the door. I could almost see everybody's heart leaping out of the shed roof so I says to this man, 'There's no need to knock that hard, Mister,' and he looks at me all cock-eyed.

'I'll knock softer then,' he says and goes tap, tap, tap, on the shed door.

'Yes?' says Karen, whipping it open.

'What?' the blind man says, looking all bewildered and Crystal by this time is leaning over the bonnet of their car choking with laughter. Why, I do not know.

The next second, whizz round the corner comes a bobby car and two bobbies leap out and stand looking at Crystal, the blind man, me and the shed.

Karen shuts the shed door very very softly.

'We heard there was an escaped shed,' one of the bobbies said heavily. 'But we didn't believe it –' and the shed suddenly lurched to its feet and went three more paces.

'Stop that shed!' roared one of the bobbies and the shed went *plonk* again on the road.

This time one of the bobbies batters on the door and Crystal slides off the side of their car laughing her head off.

'Herrrrk. Sluckslucksluck. Hoog –' she's going, trying to get her breath, I suppose.

The bobby hammers on the door again and this dim little voice shouts, ''Ello?' and the bobby goes, 'You'll get 'ello. Get this door open,' and the door grates open and there's Stella Green, standing halfway down it with Tiny at her side.

The bobby's eyes slide down and down the door until they come to Stella and then he says 'All right. Come on out. Lot of yer. Out. Out. Out,' and one by one, everybody trailed through the doorway and stood blinking in the lights of the cars.

'Great looker-out *you* are,' E.H. moans at me and I tell him, 'It wasn't my fault, Elvis. They just came.' And the bobbies looked at us and then at the shed.

'Exactly what's going on?' they asked and that was it for the rest of the night.

Karen had to fetch Mr Kendal and he nearly keeled over when he sees this shed. Then we all had to have a telling-off and then we had to wait till the bobby fetched a camera and took a picture.

Crystal, by this time, was practically stretched out on the road by their car, hissing and sobbing and roaring with laughter (too much to drink by far) and she was still at it when the blind man helped her back onto her feet, pushed her into his car and drove off.

'Blinking football team,' I snarl at Elvis H. who wasn't speaking to me because of the police.

''Ere,' raps Mr K. sharply. 'It's thanks to Lily here you ain't all mincemeat. All the same,' he goes, stroking the shed, 'this'll burn a treat.' And he went off home happy.

The only one who did, I might add.

Him – and Crystal.

Chapter Six

It was my thirteenth birthday today and I got two cards.

'Two cards!' I said to my Gran. 'Where's the rest?' And she goes back and looks under the door and there aren't any rest.

'That's all there is, my girl,' she tells me. 'Be thankful you've got two. Some folk don't get any.'

'I might as well be some folk then,' I say because it seems to me two's as bad as none.

'Happy Birthday, Lil,' E.H. tells me and I say to him, 'Fat happy birthday I'm going to have now Mr Pickle's back.'

'Wotjaget?' E.H. asked and I tell him, 'A knitted jumper off my Gran.'

'The same as last time?' he asks and I nod.

My Gran knits the worst jumpers in the world. They're only eighteen times too big for you and you practically have to keep the sleeves up with elastic bands to stop people rushing you to the hospital with missing arms.

'I haven't got anything off my Mam.'

'They'll bring you something, though,' E.H. says and I tell him I notice he hasn't sent me a card.

'Sent you a card?' he says. 'What?'

'Oh, never mind. Never mind.' But these two cards I leave at home on the sideboard and try and forget it's my birthday at all.

'What did they do with the shed?' I asked Elvis and he tells me that the bobbies helped Mr Kendal get the shed to the bonfire.

'They smashed it to smithereens,' he says. 'And carted it there in bags.'

'Football practice tomorrow,' he goes on miserably. 'I don't even want to be in this team. I hate football. Really hate it.' And he glowers at the pavement, a couple of kids and Deirdre Summers when she comes out with her triangle.

'Wanna be in my group, Elvis?' she asks.

'What kind of group is it?' E.H. asks and Deirdre whips this poster out from under her jumper.

FANS AGAINST FUR

it says.

'Nah,' Elvis tells her. 'I've got my own rock group, thanks.'

At the last count, there were three hundred

and fourteen rock groups around Rat Trap Flats, all practising in their bedrooms.

'Three hundred and fourteen, eh?' my Gran says. 'Well, I can tell you this much. It comes as no surprise to me. What! Three pairs of ear muffs a week and as for dustbin lids and cymbals, you cannot move for them.'

'Cymbals?' I ask.

'Cymbals,' my Gran says sharply. 'It's either that dratted boyfriend of yours with his terrible racket on his dustbin lids or it's the Sally Army, come to play hymns. When they pull these flats down for their police station, it'll give us all a bit of peace.'

'E.H. is breaking new ground in music, Gran,' I tell her and she sniffs and says, 'I'll be breaking new ground – with him, if he doesn't watch it. There isn't a bin with a lid on for miles around, thanks to that youth.'

'I've only borrowed your bin lid for a bit, Missis,' Elvis tells my Gran but she just snorts and says, 'Put it back on now, lad, before I lose my temper.' So E.H. fetches her bin lid back and slams it on the bin.

'They don't know good music when they hear it,' he says bitterly and I agree with him.

'A dustbin lid is meaningful,' E.H. goes on. 'It's representative.'

E.H. and the Dead Beats have to be good. When you reckon they get chucked out immediately they've played three chords wherever there's anybody over twenty, you can see you've got to be modern to like their music.

We all like it.

Well, me and Gary Smith and Mavis Jarvis and Hoggy do.

'Great,' grunts Hoggy and smashes another dustbin lid to a pulp. 'My kind of music.'

'Yer've got to 'ave sensitivity' Elvis tells him, dragging the dustbin lid away from Hoggy. 'It's no good just bashing it, Hoggy. And anyway,' he goes on, looking at this lid. 'This one's made out of rubber.'

'Ug,' says Hoggy. 'I thought there was something wrong.' And then he hangs about and hangs about until we were practically covered in cobwebs of white hair.

'Why doesn't he go home?' E.H. mutters but we don't mention this to Hoggy on account of his habit of bashing you.

'It ain't a rock group,' Deirdre grits out from between her teeth. 'Dumb kids. Dumb. Dumb.'

'Who you calling dumb?' Hoggy flashes and Deirdre tings her triangle and doesn't answer him.

Ding she goes and holds her triangle right next to her ear. *Ding. Ding* – and her triangle chimes *Ding Ding* back at her.

'Better than a budgie, really,' Karen says. 'Our budgie only goes squawk. I wouldn't mind if it went Ding.'

Elvis soon found out what this 'Fans Against Fur' group was because up comes Awful Warning with her plastic bin liners, her clogs, her Dad's pyjama jacket and her leather twenty-three years too big for her PLUS – PLUS a ratty old fox hanging round her shoulders.

'Greep,' goes Deirdre when she sees this poor old fox with his hair drifting down Peggy's bin liner. 'What is that around your disgusting neck?' she bellows.

'Whose disgusting neck?' Awful Warning shouts back wildly, looking round her for a disgusting neck.

'What?' says Asquith, sidling up behind Hoggy.

'This,' roars Deirdre, tinging away on her triangle like mad and then she stuffs it into her pocket and grabs hold of the fox's head.

Pat, Pat, she goes with her hand as gentle as patting cream.

'*This*,' she roars suddenly, frightening the life out of us. 'This poor little – sob sob – FOXY.'

'Poor little foxy,' Awful Warning repeats, looking all bewildered. 'It's a dead fox, creep. A dead as doornails fox. Ha.'

'Don't you "Ha" me,' Deirdre warns. 'Wearing a poor dead little fox around your disgusting neck,' and then she whips out her notice FANS AGAINST FUR and turns it round and pushes it into Awful Warning's green, pink, silver and lilac painted face.

MURDERER it says on the back. ANIMAL FUR ON ANIMALS.

'And,' she spits, 'you can take that how you want.'

'Are you calling me an animal?' Peggy Lane shrieks but Deirdre was too busy trying to get this dead fox from around Peg's neck to answer.

Tug, she went with this furry body and one of the fox's glass eyes dropped out at Awful Warning's feet and rolled away into the gutter, staring at us all the time.

'Aaaagh!' shrieked A.W. 'My eye. You've knocked out one of my eyes!'

'It wouldn't matter if it were one of *your* eyes,' Deirdre says fiercely. ''Cause that's only what you deserve – but it ain't your eye. It's the fox's eye.'

Snatch, she goes at this poor old fox.

Grab, old A.W. tries but the fox disappears behind Deirdre's back. I half expected to see it put its little flat paws over its ears, there was such a racket.

'What you doing with my fur?' Awful

Warning yelps. 'Give it me back. Give it me 'ere.'

'I'm liberating it,' Deirdre says meanly. 'Liberating it from you – you, you . . . murderer,' she finishes and steps back with her eyes flashing.

I never thought people's eyes really did flash. I thought that was only light bulbs but here were old Deirdre's eyes, flashing away like billy-ho.

'That fox 'as been dead a lorng time,' Gary Smith drones but Deirdre kicks him sharply on the shins.

'Shut up, Dead Beat,' she snarls. 'Dead or alive, this here fox is liberated.' But it wasn't, not for long, because old Asquith, he comes bop bopping round the pavement and liberates the fox back, then slings it round Awful Warning's disgusting neck again.

'Get lost, Ding Ding,' he tells Deirdre and she just about climbed the flat walls without touching concrete, which was just as well, considering it drops off in chunks if you so much as glance at it out of the corner of your eye.

'I'll set that fox free,' she shouts. 'You see if I don't. Murderers. Rats. Punks. Spotty Mushes!' And then she shouts 'Murderers!' once more, dings her triangle until I thought it would burst into flame and stomps away with her poster in her hand.

'Huh,' says Awful Warning, stroking her little dead fox's head. 'Creep.' And she and Asquith hoppit off, arms round each other and old Asquith's chain clanking like there's no tomorrow.

'She's got a point,' E.H. says, stroking his mushrooms but when his hand reaches them, they weren't there. They'd gone.

'Where's my mushrooms?' Elvis shouts and there's Hoggy, stuffing mushrooms into his mouth as fast as he can.

'I like mushrooms,' he grunts and snuffles the last few bits out of his hand.

'You've ate my mushrooms!' E.H. says and we all nod because we can see that's what's happened but poor old E.H. looks as if he's going to burst into tears.

Hoggy stops chomping and stares at Elvis.

'I've got a bit of chocolate,' he says at last and puts his hand in his pocket and drags out this mashed up bit of chocolate in its silver paper. 'Yer can have this, Harris, if you wants. In exchange for the mushrooms,' he finishes.

That street was littered with kids in a state of collapse, I'm not joking.

Never, in his entire history, had Hoggy Morgan given away so much as a smell of a piece of chocolate.

Elvis falls back against the wall and goes

'Nah. Nah,' because he's seen the state of that chocolate same as we have. 'It's OK, pal. You keep it. You keep it.'

'No, you 'ave some chocolate in exchange,' Hoggy insists and holds out this grotty bit of melted chocolate in its bit of silver paper.

Wham, this stick slams down from nowhere and the chocolate leaps off Hoggy's hand and falls onto the ground.

'Aaaagh!' screams Hoggy and we're all pinned to the planet in fear and terror at this great big stick appearing out of nowhere.

'Aaaagh!' screams Hoggy again but this time in black rage and he turns round slobbering at the mouth to see who's hit him and made him drop his chocolate.

And there's Mr Kendal, holding his walking stick at his side.

'I did it for your own good, lad. I think too much of you to let you go around with that muck. Nay, I couldn't just stand by and not interfere,' he says quickly, but even his face blanches when he looks at Hoggy. 'You're one of my lads,' Mr K. goes on. 'And I won't, will not, I tell you, won't stand by and watch you ruin your life. I will not. What about the football team, hey?'

'Rrrraaaaghhhh!' says Hoggy.

'Think about it,' Mr Kendal rushes on. 'The football team will be the saving of you, lad. I'd do it again,' he says and takes a step back. 'I would. I'd do it again. I'm not standing back and watching you tek them filthy drugs . . .'

'Chocolate,' bites Hoggy.

'What?' Mr K. asks.

'You made me drop my chocolate,' Hoggy growls and advances a step.

'Chocolate!' Mr Kendal says. 'Chocolate! I thought it was them filthy drugs in their filthy silver paper.'

Hoggy's eyes burned.

'It were my chocolate,' he said again and even Mr Kendal got the message this time.

'Well,' he says. 'I'm very sorry, I'm sure. Chocolate, you say?' and we all nodded. 'I wouldn't have done any different, Horace,' he sweeps on. 'No. If I thought for a second you was – or any of you was – taking them filthy drugs, I'd do the same again.'

Slobber, growl, goes Hoggy and then, all at once, his face paled and two fat tears slid out of his little red eyes.

'All right,' this voice roars. 'Who did it? Who made my Hoggy cry?' And down comes Jarvis, putting footprints into concrete with every step. 'Who did this? Who made my Hoggy cry tears?'

'I did, Mavis,' Mr Kendal says sadly. 'And I'm very, very sorry. I'd have cut off my hand rather than have made him cry. Thing is, see, I thought I was acting for the best.'

Mr Kendal put an arm round Hoggy.

'There, there lad. Don't take on so.'

'What you lot gawping at?' M.J. bellows. 'None of you ever seen anybody cry before? Come here and look in this mirror I've got. You can see somebody cry then.' And nine tenths of the kids drifted away like paper boats.

'Did I hurt thee, lad?' Mr Kendal's going and I see again that big stick slamming through the air and it makes me flinch and feel sick and breathless.

I think Mr K.'s question is the most useless thing in words that I have ever heard.

Hoggy held out his hand so we could see it and the stick must have mainly caught the chocolate because there was just a thick red mark along his fingers, not mashed up mangled bits of skin and bone that I expected to see.

'Sorry,' said Mr Kendal. 'I'm very, very sorry, Horace.'

None of us knew what to say.

'Come on. I'll take you home,' Mr Kendal said and then Hoggy started to cry harder than ever.

'Rrroooaaarrr. Rrrrroooaaarrr' he went.

'He doesn't have a home,' Mavis J. said, her

back as straight as a die and her face snow-white. 'His Mam chucked him out.'

'He doesn't have a home?' Mr Kendal repeated. 'Well, where is he living then?'

'In the boiler room at the Old People's flats,' Hoggy snuffled and all at once my two birthday cards didn't seem so bad.

They were – it's just that they didn't seem it.

'But you can't live in a boiler room,' Mr Kendal protested. 'You'd best come back with me to Mrs Kendal and we'll see what we can do to sort this mess out. My word,' he goes. 'I've never heard anything like it in my life. Living in a boiler room! Can you credit it? You can't credit it. Not at all.' And he started to hurry Hoggy forward with him.

'He's coming home with me,' he said to Mavis. 'You stop here, my girl, until I've got something sorted out. You can come and see him later on if you want.' And then they were down the pavement and crossing the street.

Hard luck on Hoggy, though, because just then Miss Sanders, striding through the flats on her flashing high heels, saw him and Mr K. and nothing would do but she must stop as well.

'Well, Morgan,' she starts. 'And what have you been doing now?' But Mr K. explains to her and they trot off together, old Hoggy between them like somebody going to the stake.

'What are you children hanging around for?' Miss S. shouts back over her shoulder. 'School, the lot of you. Anyone would think you were Lords and Ladies of Leisure to look at you. Well, you're not. Wretched children. Standing staring. You may all write . . .'

But we'd gone.

Now we're wondering what's going to happen to Hoggy and to my birthday cards.

'I'm not wondering about your stupid birthday cards,' M. Jarvis says. 'It's my Hoggy I'm bothered about. Not you.'

Who *is* bothered about me?

Nobody, that's who.

Chapter Seven

This is definitely the very last birthday I am ever having.

After school, I went back to my Gran's and as soon as I opened the door and sniffed the air, I knew that Mr Pickle and my Mam were waiting for me.

I tried to back out but my Gran, who has ears like a bat, she shouts through, 'That you, Lily?' and I have to shout back 'Yes.'

I went into the front room with my feet dragging over the carpet like anchors and there's Mr Pickle, grinning at me as if he'd never gone away when I was six and left me and my Mam for ever.

'Happy Birthday, Lily,' my Mam says quickly. 'I bet you thought we'd forgotten you. Daft thing. You should have known better. Come on, give me a hug. When are you coming back home? I miss you. We both miss you. Your Dad says you're going to think about coming back for Christmas. Is that right?'

All I could hear was 'your Dad, your Dad,' and I kept thinking, 'He's not my Dad. He's not.'

'Here,' my Mam went on. 'This is your birthday present from me.' And she gave me a white packet of tissue paper.

'What's in it?' I asked her, trying to ignore Mr Pickle.

'Open it and see, Lily,' my Mum said sharply.

I wasn't really interested in anything from my Mam or Mr Pickle seeing as how they were managing very well without me but I opened this package anyway and there were a pair of black velvet slippers with bead embroidery all over them. They were the most beautiful slippers I had ever seen in my life.

'Oh. Slippers,' I said and threw them down on the sofa. 'What's for tea, Gran?'

'A rattle round the earhole,' my Gran said thinly and gave me her fish-eye look.

I didn't say anything. I just sat down and put my lips together very very tight.

My Mum picked the slippers up and said, 'Have you noticed the embroidery, Lily? All the beads? I searched high and low for these. I knew they were what you wanted,' and she held them out to me again but I didn't take them and in the end, she threw them down on the sofa herself.

'Well, I'm off to work,' she said and she kissed Mr Pickle, shouted 'Cheerio!' to my Gran and was gone. Who cares? Not me.

'I could really shake you sometimes,' my Gran said and went banging out to the kitchen and started flinging cups through the window, it sounded like.

I felt very lonely and I had to turn right away from Mr Pickle so that I couldn't see him beaming away like some barmy light-house that hadn't been switched off.

'I have a present for you, as well,' he said now and I almost fell off my chair with boredom.

'Here,' he says and points to this enormous brown box on the floor.

'Happy Birthday, Daphne,' he goes and that made me jump.

'Aren't you going to open the box?' he says now and my Gran stalks back in from the kitchen and stands in the doorway scowling at me like thunder.

'Yeah,' I said at last and pulled at the string round this box.

Nothing happened because it must have been tied in about six thousand knots.

'Are you sure I'm supposed to open it at

all?' I asked Mr Pickle three hours later, when every finger nail I owned was lying broken on my Gran's carpet.

'Better cut it,' my Gran said and before we could blink, she'd gone snip, snip, snip with her scissors and the box was almost undone.

I ripped open the top and stared inside.

'Go on. Get it out,' Mr Pickle said. 'It's yours.' And I pulled out of that box a brand new portable television set with full colour.

'Now how did you get the money to pay for that?' my Gran asked and looked at Mr Pickle all thoughtful.

He shrugged.

'Oh, I manage,' he said and I could tell he was with my Gran like I was when I was trying to stop her poking and prodding and finding out things I didn't want her to know.

'It's very nice, Mr Pickle,' I said and Mr Pickle sighed a bit then said 'Can't you call me Dad, Daphne?'

It was my turn to shrug then and he got up and said he'd have to be going.

'Is there a plug on that dratted thing?' my Gran asked and Mr Pickle said yes, he'd put one on himself and then he was gone and the front door banged shut behind him and we could hear his feet clattering down the stairs of the flats.

I went to the window and looked down. I

wasn't bothered about Mr Pickle at all but
when he got on the pavement, he stopped and
looked back up at my Gran's and then he
waved but I didn't wave back.

As soon as he'd gone round the corner, I
was sat on the sofa pulling my shoes off and
putting on my lovely velvet slippers and all
the time my Gran was watching me.

'You should be ashamed of yourself,' she
said at last. 'Not even a word of thanks to
your poor Mam for them slippers, yet you
knew they were just what you wanted.'

Then she sighed and goes on, 'Oh well.
Selfish is as selfish does. Look, you haven't
had a birthday treat yet. How about having
one of your pals to stop the night and then
you can watch this here TV your Dad's
bought?'

'Where will *you* sleep?' I asked and my Gran
said she would sleep on the sofa for one night.

'It won't kill me,' she said. 'At least I don't
think it will.' So we took the television into
the bedroom and then I went flashing round
to ask old Karen if she'd like to come and
watch my new telly with me.

'Yers,' she said. 'That should be good.'

'You're going nowhere without Stella,' her
Mam said when she asked. 'It's our one night
out tonight, my lass, so where you go, she
goes.'

'It's not fair,' Karen started then shrugged and said to me, 'Can she come?'

I nodded.

'If she's quiet,' I said. 'My Gran won't even know she's there.' So Karen locked Tiny up and we got Stella ready and all she did was moan.

'Ohhhh, I donwannagoansleepwithLily. Iwannastayinmyownbed. Nehhhhrrrr.'

'Shut up, young Stella,' Karen bites out. 'Else I'll knock your block off and you won't bother where you sleep then.'

We trailed through the flats back to my Gran's and when we got to her front door, I put my key in the lock, pushed the door open and was going to go 'Shhhh!' when Tiny bounds out of nowhere, shoves past me and is sat on the hall carpet going, 'Woof Woof!'

'Where the blinking heck did he come from?' Karen wails.

'He'll have to go before my Gran comes back from bingo,' I tell Karen and she says, 'Stella. Tell that dratted dog to go home. Go on. Tell him –' *clip*, she goes round Stella's ear.

'Grrrrrr,' says Tiny and Stella howls and shouts 'Kill!' to Tiny and doors start opening up and down the flats.

'Come in,' I hiss. 'Before we have the entire estate up here!' And we all push in through the door with Tiny refusing to move so much as a paw.

'Get him into the bedroom,' I tell Stella and she sticks her bottom lip out, takes a deep breath and gets ready to howl again.

'One sound –' Karen puts her finger in the air, '– one sound, sister, and you're done for.'

Gulp, goes little Stella and her and Tiny stomp off into the bedroom. Clomp, clomp, clomp they go on the carpet and they look absolutely identical.

'You don't know how lucky you are not to have any brothers or sisters,' Karen says bitterly. 'Blinking kids.'

By the time we got Stella and her moaning mouth into bed, Tiny settled on the rug, me and Karen each side of Stella, it seemed like it was practically midnight.

'What'll we watch, then?' Karen says and we look at the paper. 'Here, what's this?' she goes and I have a look.

'"The Monster from the Swamp",' I read out and young Stella's eyes go big as buckets.

'Wossaswamp?' she asks.

'Oooh,' Karen goes. 'I quite like monsters. Don't you, Lily?'

The one thing I hate most in the world are monsters but I look at Karen and she looks at me and I say, 'Yeah. Monsters are great.'

Karen says, 'Right, that's what we'll watch

on your new telly, then. "The Monster from the Swamp".'

So, I get out of bed and pad across to the telly and switch it on.

'Put the light out,' Karen says. 'We can't watch a monster film with the light on.' So I put the light out and the telly suddenly screams at me and I jump clean across that bedroom floor straight into bed, I was that scared.

'Yergotyerfootinmymouth,' young Stella mutters, half asleep. 'Kill!' she tells Tiny but Tiny's standing bolt upright on the rug watching this monster come out of the swamp on telly.

'Woof!' he goes at it and me and Karen stare at the picture through our fingers.

Snore, breathes young Stella.

'Grrrrr', threatens Tiny as the monster rears up in the air.

'Aaaagh!' bellows Karen when we see his face. ''E's got fangs. Wiv blood on them,' and everything happened at once then.

'Grrrrr. Woof Woof!' Tiny barks.

'Raaaaaagh!' howls the monster on the telly.

'Eeeeeeeek!' screams the person he is busy chomping up.

All I can hear is my heart thudding. It was going so hard I thought it would push its way out of my body.

'Woof. Woof!'

'Aaaaagh!'

'Scream!'

'Eeeeeeek!'

'Grrrrrr!'

And then, through it all, there comes this voice.

'What on earth is going on here?' And there's my Gran, standing looking round the room which is absolutely jammed pack full of noise and light from the TV.

'What a racket!' she bawls and strides across the room.

'Hello.' She stops and peers at the bed. 'Who's this?' And young Stella turns over and snores again.

'Young Stella!' my Gran says in amazement. 'What on turtle (!) is she doing here?'

Then she sees Tiny and he offers her a paw.

'*And* the dog! Well, I'll be blowed. Get down!' she says to Tiny. 'Get down. You're not getting round me like that.' And Tiny plonks his huge feathery paw back down on the rug.

'Where's everybody else?' she asks Tiny and pulls the bedclothes back. 'They're not in here and that's a fact. Where are you, Lily?' she cries.

'Haaaaagh!' the monster roars and eats

somebody else.

'Dratted thing,' my Gran mutters. 'Let me put that off.' And just as she's walking past the wardrobe, Karen screams at the top of her voice and falls out onto my Gran's shoulders.

It was my Gran's turn to scream then. I thought she was going to go through the roof.

'What the . . .?' she cries and then strides across and switches off the TV, puts the light back on and says to Karen, 'Stop screaming, Karen. Be quiet. Dear me. My head's thumping. Shut up, lass!' she yells when Karen goes on screaming.

'What on earth were you doing in the wardrobe?' she asks when Karen shuts up at last.

'Watching TV,' Karen sobs and my Gran goes, 'Tut, tut,' and 'I don't know. You girls. Now then,' she says, looking round. 'That reminds me. There's somebody missing. Where are you, Lily?' she cries and I push the bedspread out of my eyes, tap her ankle and peer up from under the bed.

'Aaagh!' my Gran shouts when my fingers touch her ankle and then she glances down and sees my face staring at her. 'For goodness' sake, you lasses. You've got me as jumpy as you. Come out of there. I don't know. Watching that rubbish. You'll watch anything, I'm not jesting. It's all plasticine and tomato sauce on TV these days. And that's what we pay a licence for. Here,' she goes. 'Has your Dad got a licence for that thing?'

'I dunno,' I mutter and she hauls me up and says, 'You want locking up, Lily. Watching monsters at your age.' And that was the end of watching TV for that night.

My Gran went on and on and on until me and Karen almost climbed in through the front of the telly to pull the monster of the swamp out. He'd have been better company than my Gran and that's saying something.

'You've just done it now,' my Gran tells me. 'No more having friends in.' Then she turfs Tiny out into the kitchen and makes sure me and Karen are lying flat as boards either side of young Stella and then she switches the light off and goes out.

''Ere,' says Karen as soon as my Gran's gone. 'Do you think that monster'll come and get us?'

'It's only on the telly,' I say. 'It's not real.' But all the same, me and Karen sleep in shifts, just to be on the safe side.

By the time daylight came, my eyes felt as if they weighed a double decker bus each.

When I went into the kitchen to make a cup of tea, I nearly had a heart attack because there was Tiny, chewing my Gran's red rug like a bar of nougat.

Chomp, pull, chew, he was going. Munch, munch, and then he started all over again.

'You must be trying to get me hung,' I tell this stupid dog but he just keeps on chewing and spitting out the bits he doesn't like.

'Look what he's done to the rug!' I scream quietly at Karen who was two steps behind me.

'He's like that,' she says. 'That's why he has to sleep in a kennel – when he will, that is.'

We stuffed what was left of the rug into Karen's bag and she hauled it away with her with young Stella and Tiny.

'I think we'll erm . . . we'll go before your Gran gets up,' Karen says, eyeing these millions of little bits of red rug which were drifting over the kitchen floor and, zip, they'd gone practically whilst the door was still locked.

Just as well, because before my Gran had time to wonder about her best kitchen rug, there was a sharp rat-tatting on the door.

'Who on earth can that be,' she says, 'at this time of the morning?' And she pulls her dressing gown round her and goes through to the hall.

'Hello?' she shouts through the door and Mr Pickle answers her.

'Erm . . .' he says, 'it's me . . .' and my

Gran opened the door and in came Mr Pickle with a friend.

'Have you . . . erm . . . have you got that there TV I bought you yesterday,' he asks me and his face looks a bit like I think mine must have looked when I saw Tiny chewing my Gran's rug.

'Yes,' I tell him.

'Why?' asks my Gran and stands in front of Mr Pickle not letting him or his friend move a step. 'What do you want to know for? Eh? Eh?'

'Do you mind if we come in a bit further, so that we can shut the door?' Mr Pickle says at last and my Gran steps back about a half a centimetre and says, 'If you feel you have to.'

'Lily,' Mr Pickle says, 'have you got that television handy?'

I point to the bedroom and Mr Pickle rushes on, 'Can you fetch it for me?'

'Just a minute. Just a minute,' my Gran flashes. 'What do you want it for? Eh? That was Lily's birthday present.' And she stares at Mr Pickle's silent friend and he stares down at the floor.

'Well, to tell you the truth,' Mr Pickle starts, 'something seems to have gone wrong with the . . . erm . . . finance.'

'You haven't paid for it,' my Gran snaps and Mr Pickle's face went a bit more miserable.

'I gave 'em a deposit,' he said. 'But . . . well, they've decided I can't have any credit so . . . well . . .'

'Now, look 'ere, Missis,' Mr Pickle's pal bursts in. 'I've come to fetch the dratted thing back. It's what you call a repossession, see. I ain't got all day to stand 'ere so if you could fetch it out, I'll be on my way.'

He wasn't a friend at all.

'You've said enough,' my Gran tells this man sternly. 'More than enough.' And then she turns to me. 'Fetch that television, Lily,' she orders and when I fetch it, she says to this bloke, 'Take it. Take it.'

This man grabs it in his arms and he's just turning to rush off with it, when my Gran says, 'Just a minute, you. Not so fast. Whose is the plug?'

'Mine,' Mr Pickle says and looks like a sick canary.

Poor old Mr Pickle, I thought, and I says to this man, 'It were a rotten telly, Mister. You shouldn't be selling stuff like that. It's a good job they *are* taking it back,' I tell Mr Pickle. 'Because if he hadn't come for it, we'd have had to have sent for him. It was terrible. Terrible.'

Mr Pickle gives me a dim smile.

'I don't know about that, I'm sure,' this

man says but my Gran tells him *he* doesn't have to know, it's *we* who have to know and *we* do know and that's all that counts.

'And take that plug off before you leave this house,' she orders and the man just drags the wires out almost and flings the plug on the hall table.

I thought Mr Pickle was going to cry when my birthday present had vanished down the stairs.

'Easy come. Easy go,' my Gran says and stalks back into the room.

'I'm sorry, Lily,' Mr Pickle tells me. 'Really. I thought it'd be all right.'

'It's OK Mr Pickle,' I tell him. 'It weren't a bit of good, really. Kept us awake all night.'

'Well, I'm sorry,' Mr Pickle says again and rubs a hand over his chin, which was blue and bristly because he hadn't had time to shave.

'He's always sorry. That's his trouble,' my Gran shouts through meanly. 'I told her not to marry you and I was right. A leopard can't change its spots.'

My Dad sighed and turned away.

'I suppose not,' he said. 'Although they can try,' he finishes and stares at the middle door.

'Don't worry, Mr Pickle,' I tell him. 'I don't think I want a television of my own, anyway.'

Then Mr Pickle was gone as well.

I thought nothing had stopped for long at my Gran's that morning. Karen, Stella, Tiny, the rug, my telly and now Mr Pickle, all gone.

Easy come, easy go, all right.

Chapter Eight

By the time Mr Kendal had got us all together on the field, the other team were there too.

'Our first Home match and I'm absolutely exhausted, I am,' Mr K. goes. 'What! Getting you lot in one place at one time is enough to wear out a ham bone.'

He had us lined up pronto and this time, he had a foreign coin to throw in the air.

'Foreign coin,' he scoffed when I asked him about it. 'That ain't foreign. That's an old British penny. Hmph!' he goes. 'Right. Heads or tails?' And Mavis shouted, 'Heads!' and then tried to screw Karen's head off her shoulders to throw up with the old penny.

'Won't put up with it!' Mr Kendal roared. 'Off the pitch, Mavis. Unprovoked assault, that. Where's the cards?' And he fishes about in his pocket and drags out a handful of cards.

'There,' he cries and holds a red card in the air.

'Pretty colour, that,' Deirdre Summers says. 'Something like my new nail polish.'

Scream, goes Mr Kendal.

'That is a FINAL card,' he roars. 'Final, that's what that is. Get off, Mavis.'

'Erm,' mutters Asquith. 'The game hasn't started yet, Mr Kendal. Can you send somebody off before it's even started?'

It's a wonder steam didn't come out of Mr K.'s ears, he was that mad.

'Very well, then,' he says. 'Very well,' and he changes his red card for a yellow one.

'Nah,' goes Michelle Parrish. 'Don't like that colour.'

'You're not supposed to like it,' E.H. tells her. 'That card means "You have been warned".'

'Did you hear that, Mavis?' Mr K. asks. 'You have been warned. The very next time you try and rip Karen's head off, you'll be sent off this pitch without a word of argument. I shall have no mercy. None. Right?'

'Grunt,' goes old Mavis and pats the goal posts back into their six feet of concrete.

'Let that be a lesson to you,' Mr K. goes on. 'And another thing, this game is about honour and decency and dignity and all them things. You don't try and rip up the goal posts just because you've been warned. Right?'

'Right, Mr Kendal,' glowers Mave the mouth but I think I shouldn't like to be anybody who gets a ball into her goal.

She'd probably tear them limb from limb as well as not letting them have the ball back.

Mr Kendal threw the coin up and I shouted 'Heads!' and one of the six thousand little lads whose team we were playing shouted 'Tails!' and we were off.

Up to one end of the field me and Michelle and Deirdre ran and Mr Kendal roars at us, 'What you lot doing up there?'

'We're after the ball, Mr K.' Deirdre tells him and holds her hands out at us.

'How dim can you get?' she says. 'And he's supposed to be the Referee.'

'The ball?' says Mr K. as if he's talking to two year olds. 'The ball is down the other end of the pitch.'

'Bor-ing,' grates Michelle peevishly. 'Blinking game,' and she charges back down the field, with me and Deirdre right behind her, only to find that E.H. has kicked it back up to where we came from.

'Ooooh!' shout these lasses, stupid lasses, who are fans of E.H. and the Dead Beats. 'Look how he runs. Isn't he good!' – and E.H. forgets all about the ball, skids to a halt and starts to try and comb his non-existent hair.

'You. You!' screams Mr Kendal, racing up

to Elvis. 'This is a warning. You let that ball go without even trying to protect it.'

'Sorry,' E.H. mutters and charges off.

'Leave 'im alone,' one of these dumb lasses shouts. 'He's wonderful, is Elvis.' And all five and a half of them started to scream, 'Elvis. Elvis. WE LOVE YOU, Elvis.'

It's a wonder the entire field of players weren't sick on the spot.

Then it started to rain. You couldn't see any of us for mud. It was like playing football in a mud bath.

Mr Kendal blew his whistle and called a halt to the first half.

'Right,' he says. 'That was just ten minutes long and I have to say I have never seen worse playing in my whole life. No. Never. Not even Workton Wanderers are as bad as you lot.'

We thought that wasn't very kind because Workton Wanderers have never won a game since they were put together.

Next, Mr K. tells us we have to change sides.

This threw us into confusion, you may be sure.

'I've only just got used to this side,' Deirdre wailed and tinged her triangle.

'Give me that triangle,' Mr Kendal says but Deirdre won't. 'If I see that again, I shall send you off the pitch,' Mr K. roared and Deirdre whipped it out and tinged it twelve times but Mr Kendal pretended he hadn't seen it at all and didn't send her off.

Wheeee, Mr K. blew his whistle again and we were off. Deirdre got the ball straight away and she picked it up and wouldn't let anybody have it. The entire team of little lads were jumping up and down around her.

'I got it first,' she says calmly. 'And I am keeping it.'

Mr Kendal nearly choked on his whistle this time. I thought he was going to blow the pea straight out of the end of it.

'Put that dratted ball down, Deirdre!' he shouted.

'If you insist,' Deirdre drawls and fishes the ball out from under her jumper and then suddenly charges down the field with it in front of her feet.

'Not that way. Not that way!' Awful Warning screams at her but Deirdre was going full pelt.

'Look at meeeeeeeeee,' she's yelling. 'Look at meeeeeeee –' And all these little lads and our team were looking at her for all they were worth.

'GOAL' screams Deirdre as she slams the ball into the net like a proper footballer. 'G–O–A–L!' And she jumps up and down in the rain, beaming and grinning and Asquith sits down on the ground and starts going sob-sob, sob-sob.

'Hurray. Hurray!' shouts the other team. 'Well done. Great goal that,' and Deirdre's shaking hands with them and getting patted on the back until she suddenly realises there's something wrong.

''Ere,' she says. 'You're the wrong team. You shouldn't be cheering.' And these little lads were dancing with joy.

'You're dumb, you are,' Asquith sobs at her. 'Dumb. You've only gone and scored an own goal.'

Mavis Jarvis's eyebrows nearly vanished onto Mars, she was that surprised.

'Should I have stopped that ball?' she says and Mr Kendal picks himself off the ground where he has been beating his head, and he shouts, 'Stopped that ball! Should you have stopped that ball! Dear me,' he roars and falls onto his knees and looks up at heaven, which was pretty wet. 'Tell me what to do?' Mr Kendal goes on as if he were praying and none of us knew whether to clasp our hands together and close our eyes or what.

But then he struggles to his feet and starts shouting again.

'The next time I see you leaning against the goal post watching a ball go into your own goal, Mavis, you will be finished with this team. Finished. And as for you, Deirdre,' he snarled, 'a fat lot of help you've turned out to be – scoring an own goal.'

Deirdre scowled.

'Does it matter?' she says. 'I thought the important thing was to get the ball into the back of a net – any net.' And then she takes out her triangle and plays 'One man went to mow' on it and refused to speak to anyone else at all.

Mr Kendal said he had lost heart for the whole game and just wished he hadn't booked a 'Friendly' match against Workton Wanderers Junior Second Team.

Asquith said we'd surely know what we were doing by then and it was all Mr Kendal's fault anyway for allowing lasses into the team in the first place.

Mr K. fixed Asquith with a stare as cold as ice-cream.

'Before you start complaining, lad, take that dratted chain off that fastens your two good legs together.'

'Never,' says Asquith and runs back down the field with tiny little steps so that he looked like a wind-up toy stuttering through the mud.

We played for another three minutes and Mr Kendal blew his whistle *again*.

'You don't get long at it, do you?' Karen says and we all shook our heads.

'All right, Mavis,' Mr Kendal says wearily. 'All right. Get 'im down.'

Mavis lifted her eyebrows again.

'Get 'im down, I say,' Mr Kendal went on and finally, Mavis lifted this little lad down who she'd draped over the top goal post.

'If I ever see you in front of this goal again, I shall toss you up in the air and swat you into the middle of next week,' Mavis tells this little lad.

'I'm the Captain of our team,' this lad bellows and starts complaining like nobody's business to Mr Kendal.

'You are not allowed to put footballers over the top of the goal,' Mr K. says coldly and each word seemed to turn into ice as it came out of his mouth and fell tinkling to the ground.

'Sorry, I'm sure,' M.J. shrugged and the little captain said he was going to report Mavis to everybody in the entire world.

'Play on. Play on,' Mr Kendal says impatiently and blows his whistle again and then just as E.H. was pelting full blast down the pitch with the ball, he happened to look up and that stopped him in his tracks, I can tell you. There was a long skid mark behind him.

'What's that?' E.H. says to Mr Kendal who has come running up.

'What?' asks Mr K. peering through the rain that was bouncing off his face.

'That,' says E.H. and points and the whole of the two football teams stare at the wall at the end of the field, which is starting to be knocked down by some men with yellow hats on.

'Well, by gah,' says Mr Kendal in astonishment. 'What the . . .?' And before he can say another word, behind the men comes roaring a big yellow earth-moving machine.

'They've come to start the new road,' Elvis tells Mr K. and we all stand, feeling miserable and really fed-up as the men and the big earth machine come rumbling onto the football field.

'They don't care,' Mr Kendal says suddenly. 'They just don't dratted well care.' And he took off his cap, wrung it out and then slapped it back on his head.

'You votes for them and what do they do? They lets you down,' he sort of half wailed. 'They lets you down and takes away yer only football field.' And then he went rushing up to the men in their yellow helmets.

'Where are these kids going to play now?' he shouts.

'Erm . . .' go the men and trudge off

behind the yellow machine and we all went and stood with Mr Kendal in the rain.

'Come on, men,' he says at last. 'Let's go and get changed.' And we trailed off that field across to the Old People's Centre to get changed.

Splodge, splodge, splodge we went down the pavement and across the road.

Mr Kendal knocks on the door of the Old People's Centre and the new Warden comes and stands looking at us.

''Ave you seen what they're doing on that field?' Mr K. asks the Warden and she sniffs. 'I'm going to get a petition up, that's what I'm going to do,' and we were all milling around him with our soggy bodies and splodgy clothes.

'I 'opes you don't think that mucky lot's coming in 'ere?' the Warden says suddenly and Mr Kendal rears up and stares at her furiously.

'Certainly they are,' he says. 'I 'ad an arrangement with the last Warden.'

'Well, you ain't got an arrangement with this one,' the new Warden snaps and closes the door – *clip* – right in front of our noses.

'I'll be danged,' Mr Kendal says. 'What's the world coming to – I ask you?' and he looks at us.

E.H. wipes the mud out of his eye and is

just going to answer when Mr K. goes on, 'Come on. Back to my flat. Don't let them get you down, eh? Mrs Kendal won't turn you away just because you're a bit damp with a little bit of muck on you.'

We looked at each other and we were soaking wet through and so caked with mud, you could hardly tell who was who. All except for Asquith with his chains, Awful Warning with her spikes and Elvis Harris with his stupid fans.

Whizz, the door opens again and the new Warden stands there with her arms folded.

'Very well,' she says. 'Very well. You can come in just this once and then . . . then, no more. No more.'

We trooped into the Centre and got washed off and changed and Mr Kendal had a look at E.H.'s tooth which had come loose.

'Dentist for thee, lad,' he said and I was glad when E.H.'s face went white.

'Ooooh!' simpers one of the birdbrains he calls fans. 'Let me kiss it out for you, Elvis.'

Mavis Jarvis offered to knock it out and me, I said nothing at all and probably won't speak to Harris for at least three years.

Fans!

Huh!

Chapter Nine

My Mam came round to my Gran's this morning and she said, 'Well, that's it, Lily. I want you to come back with me. Your Dad's right upset about his telly.'

'It weren't his telly,' my Gran put in smartly. 'It was Lily's.'

'I know, mother,' my Mam said. 'All the same, I want her to come home. Her Dad's getting very depressed.'

It was then I noticed my Gran fetching out two carrier bags full of my clothes. I couldn't help but notice because she dumped them in the middle of the carpet and said, 'Now, my girl. It's clear to me you should be with your Mam and Dad. What I thought was that you could come and sleep here at weekends,' and that was how it was agreed between them but it wasn't agreed with me. Not at all.

We walked home and Mr Pickle made room for me on the sofa so that I could sit and have my breakfast and then he said, 'We thought we might have a puppy,' and I thought of Tiny and said, 'I don't want no puppy.'

'Goldfish?' said Mr Pickle.

I shook my head.

'Canary? Budgie? Parrot? Cat? Kitten? Black mamba?'

'What?'

'A black mamba. My, they're very interesting pets.'

'What are they?' I ask him and he hums and hahs and tuts and then he says, 'Snakes.'

'Snakes!' I say and think I'd have been better to have had the puppy whilst I had the chance.

'You're not getting a black mamba or any other colour of mamba,' my mother said quickly. 'There's no snakes coming in here.'

She was quite wrong though because just then E. Harris knocked on our front door and when I opened it and saw him, I said, 'My Mam said "No snakes" so buzz off, Harris.'

'Stop messing about, Lil,' E.H. went. 'I've got terrible toothache. It weren't my fault them lasses were there. They were only my fans,' he went and practically preened himself in the door handle.

'Huh!' I said but E.H. just winced as his tooth started to ache again.

'Aaaargh,' he groaned. 'You should be in my mouth just now.'

'Blerkkk,' I said. 'First my Dad . . . erm . . . Mr Pickle offers me a black mamba and then you . . .'

'What's a black mamba?' E.H. asked and I told him, 'A snake.'

'That sounds interesting. When's he getting it?'

'He isn't getting it. My Mam says no snakes in the house so that lets you out, don't it. Goodbye and cheerio.'

Just then old E.H. went chalk white and clutched at the door post for support.

''Ere, Lily,' he mumbles. 'What am I going to do about my tooth?' And my Mam came out, took one look at E.H. and says, 'Come on in, lad. Fancy you letting him stand at the door, Lily. You can see he's not well.'

E.H. tottered into the front room and collapsed on the sofa, holding his face in his hands.

'It's me tooth,' he said to Mr Pickle.

'I 'ad a tooth like that,' Mr Pickle starts. 'When I was . . . what . . . your age. Yeah, must have been and I had to go to the dentist and have it out.'

'So's Harris,' I tells him. 'He has to go to the dentist this afternoon.'

'I ain't going,' E.H. mumbles and Mr Pickle

looks all sorry for him.

'Why, it won't hurt a bit,' he says. 'The worst bit's the needle. After that, it's a picnic. 'Course,' he goes on, 'my tooth was very deep. I remember it well. The dentist had to get a soap box and stand on that so he could pull it out better.'

By this time, E.H.'s face was light green and covered in sweat.

'Let's go out,' he says to me, all sickly and sorrowful, so I got my coat and we went out into the flats.

'I ain't going to no dentist,' E.H. moans when we get into the open. 'Your Dad's useless, Lil. "The worst bit's the needle." Huh. I don't need to be told that.'

'I had a tooth out and it didn't hurt me,' I tell him and he says that's probably because I'm a girl. (!)

'Nah,' he goes on. 'What I thought we'd do would be to wait till your Mam goes out and then go back to your house and we could pull this tooth out ourselves.'

I practically went slap backwards.

'I'm not fishing around in your grotty mouth,' I tell Elvis but he rushes on, 'Don't be so daft. What we're going to do is tie this string –' (and he fishes out a long bit of white string) '– around my tooth, fasten it to the door handle and then you can slam the door.'

'And what'll happen?' I ask him and he almost jumps up and down with rage and pain.

'What'll happen? What'll happen?' he yells and then flinches as the cold air zips into his mouth and yanks at his bad tooth. 'Aaaagh! What'll happen . . . yelp . . . is that this blinking tooth . . . wheeee . . . will shoot out and that'll be . . . aaaagh . . . that.'

'Oh,' I say.

By the time our flat is empty, E.H. is practically weeping in agony and no sooner had I got the front door open than he rushes inside and starts trying to tie his string to his bad tooth.

'Yahhh!' he's going. 'Ouch. Yelp!'

'Wouldn't it be easier to go to the dentist?' I ask but he shakes his head, mutters, 'Nohg, it wonk.'

'Pardon?' I say.

'Nohg, it wonk!' he shrieks. 'Tig the strig to the dog ongle.'

'Right,' I tell him and take hold of this mucky bit of string he hands me.

Then I tie it round the door handle and stand back.

'Ohg the dog,' E.H. yelps.

'What?' I ask and stare at him.

'Ohg the dog then . . . then slav it shug. Aaaagh!' he finishes, clutching his mouth.

'How do you know you've tied the bit of string to the right tooth?' I ask and Elvis Harris almost faints away with horror.

'Tig the strig to the hong terf?' he yelps. 'Dohg be stugid.'

'It's your mouth,' I tell him. 'Glad it ain't mine,' I mutter as I open the door.

'Stand back,' I say and go, 'One . . . two . . . three!' and slam the door shut with all my might.

I asked E.H. afterwards if he's ever considered taking up the high jump but he just snarled 'Nohg!' because, I'm not kidding, he leapt across after that door as if he were a tennis ball on wings.

Zoom, he went and ended plastered to the wood.

'That's no good,' I tell him. 'Your tooth won't come out that way.' And E.H. peels himself off the door and he's going, 'Snerf. Snerf. I'g feg ut, I'g am. Feg ut.'

'Then you shouldn't have jumped when I shut the door,' I tell him. 'You should stand still and when the door shuts, zip –' and E.H. winced, '– out will come your tooth.'

'Rihg,' he says and we start all over again but it was no good.

The harder I slammed the door, the higher and faster E.H. jumped until I shouted, 'One last time, E.H. and that's all. Now, stand still –' because thirty-six windows had dropped straight out of their holes since I'd started.

I took a deep breath, opened the door and stood well back.

Wham, I slammed it shut, looked round and E.H. had gone. Vanished.

'Where are you, Elvis?' I shouted. 'Speak to me.' And this faint little voice comes through the door, 'I'g erg.'

'What?' I cried.

'I'g erg,' it comes again.

Well, I looked all round and there wasn't anything to be seen, only this long bit of mucky string dangling from the door handle.

Slowly, I opened my Mam's front door and peered through the crack at the side.

'How did you get there?' I asked because there, on the other side of the door, is E.H.

'My toog,' he's crying. 'Dengist, thak's ogs there igs to ig. Dengist!' And he starts staggering off down the passage and won't even wait for me to catch him up.

'Dengist,' I hear him wailing right down the stairs. 'Dengist. Dengist . . .' and then he was gone.

'I never even saw him,' I told my Mam afterwards. 'He must have gone past me like a flash of lightning.' And we both stared into the washing-up water without speaking, we were so overcome.

'But he never takes any exercise,' my Mam said and I nodded.

'I know.'

I didn't see E.H. again until Monday when we were back at school.

'Are you all right?' I asked him and he just turned round and said, 'Don't speak to me. If you'd slammed that door right, I wouldn't have had to have gone to the dentist at all.'

'If you hadn't jumped,' I told him, 'your tooth would have been hanging off our front door on a bit of string.' And then we had to stop talking on account of Miss Sanders prowling the classroom and snipping, 'Where's Morgan? Does anybody know where Morgan is? You, Jarvis. Are you bursting with information?'

'Bursting with nothing,' says this voice and M. Jarvis flashes round in her desk ready to make mincemeat out of Karen.

'Fifty lines, Green,' Miss Sanders says, without hardly drawing breath. 'One more word and you shall be the Spirit of Christmas standing in the Hall by the Christmas tree for the next two days.'

That certainly shut old Karen up. Nobody in their right mind wants to be the Spirit of Christmas.

'Hair?' Miss Sanders goes on. 'Is that hair on your head, Harris?'

E.H. nods.

'Hair today and gone tomorrow, I suppose?' Miss Sanders goes on and then laughs at her own terrible joke. 'Ha, Ha,' she says. 'Note children, that when we laugh, we laugh quietly, discreetly. Not –' *swat*, she goes to Awful Warning, '– in a raucous and most unladylike manner. And remove that dead fox from around your neck, Lane.'

''AveIgorrerpleaseMissaveI?' says old Peg and Miss Sanders whips this poor old fox off and slams it on her desk.

'I do not argue, Lane,' she says wearily. 'I order. Now, where is its eye?'

'What?' says Peg.

'Its eye,' Miss Sanders says clearly. 'The fox is without an eye. Do not look to me for it, child, when this poor animal is returned to you.'

Slap, she goes on the fox and the other eye jumps straight out and rolls under the desk. This is one very old fox.

'Tut, tut,' goes Miss S. 'Most unfortunate.'

'Yer lost me eye,' wails A.W.

Ding ding, goes Deirdre on her triangle.

'That ain't your eye, either,' she shouts. 'It's the fox's eye.'

'Silence, Summers,' Miss S. says smartly. 'Animals are not allowed in the class-room . . .'

'Git out, Jarvis,' Karen mutters.

'Dead or alive,' Miss Sanders ripples on. 'And you, Green, will now be the Spirit of Christmas. Collect your halo from Miss Michaels, if you please, and remove yourself to the stage next to the Christmas tree, where you may practise . . .' and then she stopped because in came Hoggy Morgan, blundering about the desks like a hippopotamus.

'Late, I see, Morgan,' she spits and Hoggy says 'Yers, Miss,' and that was that.

No lines. Nothing.

It turns out that Hoggy's still living at Mr Kendal's and Mrs Kendal has had to stand on street corners with a tin plate asking for money because Hoggy has eaten everything but the pantry door.

'I tell you no lie,' she told my Gran. 'He's eaten the lot. Everything. We've had to put a lock on the fridge door. Why, we'll end up in the workhouse at this rate.'

'Won't his Mam take him back?' my Gran asked her and Mrs Kendal says, 'The woman's got more sense. No, no,' she goes on. 'I didn't mean that. It's just that . . . well . . . he does take some feeding and no mistake.'

Hoggy said at playtime that he'd got a Social Worker all to himself and she was going to work things out between his Mam and him.

'Ho, yes,' he says. 'I shall probably be back home before you can blink.'

But meanwhile, he went on, did anybody want to give him their dinner?

Two hundred voices shouted *No*.

'Smash yer faces in if yer don't,' Hoggy threatens the school and at last Mavis J. gives him her half a loaf and herd of cows which are her sandwiches.

'Meat!' spits Deirdre. 'Swines,' she goes and stomps out of the hall.

Miss Sanders lost the dead fox. When we got back in the afternoon there was nothing on her desk but a tuft of fur.

Awful Warning wept buckets.

'That were my fox,' she sobs. 'I'm gonna flatten you, Summers' she threatens Deirdre but Deirdre just smiled her little sly smile and said nothing.

'I am certain – certain it will turn up safely,' Miss S. says balefully, giving Deirdre a look which almost instantly turned her to salt. 'Meanwhile, Lane, keep this eye safely in your pocket,' and she throws the poor old fox's eye to Awful Warning.

That made us all feel so bad, we decided animals were much better keeping their eyes in their heads.

'And had we done the same,' Miss Sanders

says, 'the fox would not be missing.'

Mr Kendal said it was a lesson we could all benefit from especially on Saturday afternoon when we were playing the 'Friendly' match he had arranged with Workton Wanderers Junior Football Team.

'What!' he says. 'You'll need eyes in the back of your head if you're to beat them, that is for sure.'

We practised 'Silent Night' ready for the Carol Service before we went home and I couldn't help thinking that here I was, two weeks before Christmas and I'm playing football, living with a strange man who keeps saying he's my Dad and a Mam who cannot see we were better off on our own.

I think, 'Silent Night'? If you ask me, it were only silent because they were all in the middle of fields.

They should have come to Rat Trap Flats. They'd have had to have rewritten that carol then.

Noisy night. Awful Night.
Nothing's calm. Nothing's bright.
I wish I was in the middle of a field waiting for Jesus.

This is the noisiest place in the world and there's nowhere you can get a bit of peace.

Nowhere – thanks to Mr Pickle.

Chapter Ten

E. Harris tried to get out of playing in the Friendly because of his tooth.

'See that?' he says to Mr Kendal and opens his mouth wide enough to drive the Channel tunnel through.

'What?' asks Mr K.

'That hole, there,' fumes E.H. jabbing the air with his finger. 'That big hole.'

'Oh, *that* big hole. Yers, well, what about it?' Mr Kendal asks, peering darkly into E.H.'s mouth and that's not a job everybody would do, and E.H. tells him there is no way at all that he can play football after *surgery*.

'You ain't 'ad no surgery,' Mr K. roars. 'You've only had a tooth out. On your way, Elvis. Well, I am disappointed in you, lad. I am. I expected better.'

'Worth a try,' Elvis H. says but it was only a try because Saturday afternoon found us trudging our way to the football field, past the yellow bulldozers and earth-removers, past the men in their yellow hats and flasks of tea in their hands, past all our fans, which included my Mam and Mr Pickle.

''Ere,' Gary Smith nudges me. 'Ain't that your new Dad?' and he points to this small hill of blue and white scarves, rosettes, rattles, sashes, hats, and there in the middle of it is Mr Pickle's face which is grinning like billy-ho.

'Blue and white aren't our colours,' I say to Gary but Mr Pickle comes flaring and blowing down the field and says, 'I haven't got any red and white things, Daphne, so I thought these would do instead.'

'Yeah,' I say.

'Give us a kiss then,' Mr Pickle goes and I think I'd rather fall into a pit of hungry alligators but then I found myself giving him a kiss.

'Yuk,' I went as soon as I came to my senses but Mr Pickle just shouts, 'Go on, lass. Show 'em how to play football.' And he goes back down the field and I can hear him telling everybody, 'My lass is in this, you know. Ho yes. She's centre forward.'

'Didn't know you were called Daphne, Lil,' Gary drones but then we were at the windbreak where our team had its headquarters.

'About time.' Mr Kendal's head pops up over the orange and white stripes.

Nobody seems to have anything in red and white.

'Come on, then. Come and get yourselves ready.' And we went behind the windbreak two at a time and came out in our shorts and our shirts which we had borrowed from the school team.

Mine were that much too big for me, Mrs Kendal had to pin me together.

We had a bit of a problem with Asquith when he turned up.

'Take your chain off, lad,' Mr K. said and when Asquith opened his mouth, he said quickly, 'To put your shorts on. I've heard quite enough about freeing the people, thank you. I just wish you'd free your poor old legs.'

Asquith sniffed and looked down at his jeans which were pinned and botched together on his legs.

Then he went behind the screen and when he came out, he'd put his shorts on top of his jeans and his chain was fastened just as before.

''Ow you going to run down the pitch with your legs chained together?' Mr Kendal sobbed but Asquith just made sure his diamond earring was safe and told Mr Kendal not to worry.

'I have ways,' he said and Mr Kendal said if there was one thing that made him sicker than another, it was people who chained their legs together when they were playing football.

'Have you seen the other team?' Mavis Jarvis comes thumping up.

We all peered over the top of the windbreak to look at this other team and Tiny pushed his way into the middle, so it got a bit hairy and very very smelly and we stared at Workton Wanderers Junior Second Team.

'They don't look like no kids to me,' E.H. says, his cheeks pale.

'Well, they are,' Mr Kendal said un-certainly. 'They said it was their second chil-dren's team.' And we all stared bleakly at ninety-three giants roaring and laughing on the other side of the pitch, all except M. Jarvis and Hoggy Morgan. They were every bit as big as the other lot.

It started to snow and a referee came bounding out of the snowflakes, onto the field, blowing his whistle, checking his cards and nodding to Mr Kendal.

'Onto the pitch then, you lot,' Mr K. roars and we jogged out to our places.

Asquith had to move with a half-leaping, half-stuttering run to get to his place.

The referee looked at him as if he were a kangaroo.

Wheee, his whistle went and we were off.

That football pitch was full of giants but

Deirdre got the ball and hared down the field with it in her arms. She wasn't best pleased when the referee made her give it back to the other side.

'But it's my ball,' she protested, while we all kicked the ground, looked at the sky and wondered if Deirdre had any brains at all.

'Give it 'em back,' Asquith told her in the end. 'You never learn, Ding Ding. That ball ain't a bag of shopping, you know. STOP PICKING IT UP!'

Bang, bang, bang, went the giants and them and the ball were stood right in front of our goal.

'Rrroooaaarrrr,' goes old M.J. and, big as they were, they all took a step back.

Hoggy Morgan went charging in with his boots flying and Asquith went bop bop bopping down the field, Awful Warning bounced up and down yelling, 'To me. To me!' and then a giant kicked the ball and it landed in the back of the net.

Our net.

Mavis Jarvis came out of the goal like a torpedo. She went *swoosh* at this poor old giant and started dancing on his face with her boots.

The referee nearly turned green. He flew down the field and Mave bent down and said 'Sorry,' her laces had come undone and she hadn't noticed this giant's face lying upside down on the pitch.

'Right underneath your feet?' snarled the ref.

'Ho, yes,' M.J. says, all surprised. 'An' I never saw 'im.'

The referee showed her the yellow card and Mr Kendal zoomed onto the pitch and told Mave one more foul and she would never ever play in one of his teams again.

'Never!' he shouted. 'This is a game, not a war. Huh!' he went and stalked off the pitch.

Karen Green got the ball, raced down the field, headed it to Awful Warning who leapt into the air and headed it into the snow. Two entire teams stood waiting for it to come down out of the sky.

'Well, it went up . . .' says a giant and we all look up and the snow puthers down and covers our eyebrows and there's no sign at all of this ball.

'Erherm,' coughs Peg. 'Sorry about this,' she goes and fishes the football off her spikes.

'*Sssssssssssstt*,' goes the ball.

'Dang me!' shouts the referee. 'You've spiked it.' And Awful Warning raises an eyebrow and wanders over to Michelle Parrish.

'Fetch a new ball,' the ref yelps and when that gets thrown onto the pitch, the giants tear away with it and slam another goal into the back of our net.

'Heh, heh,' they were chortling. 'Heh, heh,' and Hoggy Morgan sidled up to one of them and breathed over his haircut.

'*Intimidation*,' screeched their manager but the referee waved the game on and Michelle Parrish took the ball from Gary the Dead Beat, flipped onto her hands and whistled the ball down the field on her feet, which happened to be resting on the wrong end of the planet.

'Foul. Foul!' the giants roar and one of them gets hold of Michelle and plonks her the right way up.

'Hands!' cries Elvis and the referee blows his whistle and the giant has to let Michelle go.

'Do you mind?' Michelle squawks and Asquith bops up on the outside, stutters a little way and then kicks the ball with both feet and it goes banging into the back of the giants' net.

Our fans went crazy. Mr Pickle nearly got separated from his voice, he was shouting so loud. Thirteen girls rushed onto the pitch and threw rice and paper flowers at Asquith.

One of the lads went flying over, jumped on Asquith's back and tried to kiss him.

I thought old Asquith was going to have a fit. He shook this lad off and went stomping up the field shouting, 'Gerrofferme. Gerroff-erme. WotdjafinkIam? Yer don't kiss Revolutionaries.'

Elvis sneered and checked his brain so that he could tell Asquith he wasn't a Revolution-ary at all.

'Dumbo,' he shouts in a fury. 'A Revolu-tionary don't wear his hair in spikes and his legs in chains.'

Asquith turned, twisted his sparkling ear-ring and said, 'Who scored the goal, Harris? You or me?' and sauntered down the field, waving like a piece of the Royal Family to all these cheering people.

In the end, when we were all looking like snowmen, the game was stopped and the referee said there would have to be a return match as soon as possible.

'What's the score?' he asks and Mr Kendal says sourly, 'Thirteen – One' and the one was ours.

'Hmmmm,' said the ref. 'A close run thing, eh?' and the giants were gloating and laughing as they made their way off the pitch.

Mr Kendal had to make Mavis Jarvis unthread a giant who had scored a goal because Mavis was trying to weave him into the football net.

''E cheated,' she says. 'And them as cheats, 'as to pay the price,' and she yanks his leg through another bit of net.

'Unthread that lad this minute,' Mr Kendal orders and M.J. sighs heavily.

We collected all our things. Took down the windbreak. Rescued Asquith from eight of E.H.'s fans, tried to thaw Michelle's hands out, which were blue with cold because she'd played the entire match on them instead of her feet. Straightened Awful Warning's spikes which had got bent with the football. Fished Karen Green practically out of Tiny's jaws. Made Hoggy Morgan stop trying to part a giant's hair with his teeth and showed Gary the Dead Beat where Elvis was explaining to the road men that he was setting up a gig with a difference and would they like to come and bring their big yellow machines with them?

'The music,' Elvis says. 'Think of the music. Man made. Man played. Meaningful to the . . . to the WORLD!' he yelled and threw a white helmet in the air.

'DESTRUCTION!' he bellows. 'Pain. Agony. Tearing into the planet. The earth screaming. The earth shrieking. The concert of the CENTURY!'

'Is he all right?' Mr Kendal asks suddenly, the windbreak under one arm, the football under the other.

'DESTRUCTION. LEGALISED VAN- DALISATION. THE END OF THE

WORLD!' Elvis roars and spins round, his eyes flashing, his face brilliant with excitement.

'THE END OF THE WORLD IN MUSIC!' he cries and the giants stare at him.

'Yes, well. Time to go home, Elvis,' Mr K. says and looks round the field.

There was only Mr Pickle in the middle of his blue and white hill. Everyone else had packed and gone.

The big yellow machines were quiet.

Mr Kendal looked at them and at us and he bounces the football on the ground.

'We'll find a new field,' he says. 'Nothing's going to stop us now. Nothing. We'll be back.' And then he starts shouting, 'Ho yes, we'll be back all right and next time . . . next time we'll beat 'em to smithereens. Smithereens, Lily.'

And I expect we will, really.

Here are some more
Young Lions
for you to enjoy:

On holiday in Romania, Paul and Judy find a small vampire under a stone. Vlad is vegetarian and all alone in the world, so the children smuggle him home, but it isn't long before they discover how much trouble even a harmless vampire can cause.

Vlad the Drac	£1.75
Vlad the Drac Returns	£1.95
Vlad the Drac Superstar	£1.75
Vlad the Drac Vampire	£1.75
Vlad the Drac Down Under	£1.75

By Ann Jungman

To order direct from the publisher, just tick the titles you want and fill in the order form on the last page.

Here are some more
Young Lions
for you to enjoy:

Simon's friend, the Witch, is loud and outrageous and has a mean-looking cat called George. As she causes confusion at the local constabulary, disrupts the local fete, goes house-hunting or takes a day trip to France, Simon discovers that with the Witch for a friend, life is never dull.

Simon and the Witch	£1.75
The Return of the Witch	£1.75
The Witch of Monopoly Manor	£1.75
The Witch on Holiday	£1.75
The Witch V.I.P.	£1.75
Simon and the Witch in School	£1.75
The Witch and the Holiday Club	£1.75

By Margaret Stuart Barry

To order direct from the publisher, just tick the titles you want and fill in the order form on the last page.

Young Lions

The Paddington Books

Michael Bond

Paddington is a *very* rare bear indeed! He'd travelled all the way from darkest Peru (with only a jar of marmalade, a suitcase and his hat) when the Brown family first met him on Paddington Station. Since then their lives have never been quite the same . . . for things just seem to *happen* to Paddington – chaotic things.

What *other* bear could turn his friend's wedding into an uproar by getting the wedding ring stuck on his paw? Or glue himself to his dancing partner's back with his marmalade sandwich? *Only* Paddington . . . but as he says himself, 'Oh dear, I'm in trouble again.'

'Within a comparatively short time, Paddington has joined Pooh as one of the great bears of children's literature.'
The Teacher

Paddington's own particular brand of chaos comes up often in Lions – in *A Bear Called Paddington, More About Paddington, Paddington Goes to Town, Paddington Helps Out, Paddington at Large, Paddington Abroad, Paddington Takes the Air, Paddington Marches On, Paddington at Work, Paddington on Top, Paddington Takes the Test, Paddington's Blue Peter Story Book* and *Paddington on Screen*.

My Best Fiend

Sheila Lavelle

"My best fiend is called Angela Mitchell and she lives in the house next door." There is nothing unusual about this opening description Charlie Ellis gives of her best friend – except the spelling – but the tales that follow reveal the very unusual scrapes these two friends seem to get into.

Pretty Angela's marvellous ideas usually lead to disaster. Like the time they got stuck on a single-track railway bridge over the River Thames with the rattle of train wheels getting closer and closer; and the time Angela accidentally caught an escaped circus lion in the back garden. But when Angela suggests burning down her dad's garage so that he could claim the insurance for a new one, Charlie really thought things had gone a bit too far. For somehow it's always Charlie who ends up taking the blame, and the spelling mistake in her English essay really wasn't much of a mistake at all.

What Difference Does It Make, Danny?

Helen Young

Danny Blane's name cropped up in a conversation between two teachers. "He doesn't look like an epileptic, does he?" commented one. "What do you expect?" came the answer. "Horns? He doesn't look like a little devil either, but he can be."

That was the point. Danny was a perfectly ordinary boy, rather better at sports than most, but, unlike most, he had epilepsy. It didn't bother him in any way until he came across a teacher who was frightened of it, and banned Danny from swimming and from using all the equipment he enjoyed most in the gym. Danny retaliated by becoming, briefly, the naughtiest boy in the school, until his problem was solved for him in a completely unexpected and dramatic way.

Every day children tackle handicaps far greater than Danny's but will nevertheless get the most out of life if expected and encouraged to do so.

Flossie Teacake's Fur Coat
Flossie Teacake – Again!

Hunter Davies

What Flossie wanted most in the world was to be a teenager like her sister Bella, to be tall and thin and wear make-up and jangling earrings and dye her hair pink.

Flossie, ten years old, tries on Bella's fur coat, and suddenly all her dreams begin to come true. A series of wonderful adventures for Flossie, exuberantly told and matched by Laurence Hutchins's lively illustrations.

All these books are available at your local bookshop or newsagent, or can be ordered from the publishers.

To order direct from the publishers just tick the titles you want and fill in the form below:

Name _____

Address _____

_____

Send to: Collins Children's Cash Sales
　　　　　PO Box 11
　　　　　Falmouth
　　　　　Cornwall
　　　　　TR10 9EN

Please enclose a cheque or postal order or debit my Visa/Access –

Credit card no:

Expiry date:

Signature:

– to the value of the cover price plus:

UK: 60p for the first book, 25p for the second book, plus 15p per copy for each additional book ordered to a maximum charge of £1.90.

BFPO: 60p for the first book, 25p for the second book, plus 15p per copy for the next 7 books, thereafter 9p per book.

Overseas and Eire: £1.25 for the first book, 75p for the second book. Thereafter 28p per book.

Young Lions